Space K
Journey of Hope

Alan Nettleton

Second edition.

Cover artwork by: darrya__

Chapter One
Message

Friday 23rd November 2068, 2:39 am

Sophie Williams floated in cool water. Bright light shimmered through a blur from above, but she could see little else. Somehow, she could breathe slowly and deeply even though she was fully submerged. Muffled blooping sounds made her feel relaxed and peaceful, like a baby in a womb.

Then she realised; she had been here before.

Oh no.

The peace was interrupted by a sudden, crystal clear voice. *"Sophie!"*

Cold, scaly fingers grasped her hand from behind. She flinched and turned. A wavy outline of a head and bright yellow eyes floated in front of her. Her breathing quickened.

"Sophie!"

Who are you? What are you? Why do I keep coming back here?

Sophie tried to focus on the creature through the watery haze. The head looked too big for the body, and the eyes too big for the head. It appeared more reptile than human. Those large, yellow eyes were drawing her in.

"Sophie, come to us. Help us."

How can I help you? What do you want from me?

A second later, Sophie was no longer underwater. Squinting in the bright sunlight, she stood on a hill, overlooking a strange landscape dominated by impossibly tall trees covered in purple flowers. Majestic dragon-like creatures with aeroplane-sized wings soared over them.

Oh no! Not the rocks. Please, I don't want to see them.

The air thinned as the wind picked up. The dragons, which previously glided effortlessly in formation, started scattering. Some darted left, some right, whilst others hovered and stared at the sky. They seemed to be panicking as if they knew something terrible was about to happen.

Sophie followed the gaze of the dragons staring upwards. A ball of light was expanding, accompanied by a screeching whistle. The light continued to grow until replaced with an almighty, blinding flash and a thunderous explosion. Dozens of fireballs began obliterating the purple trees, pelting the surface and sending plumes of smoke and debris into the air. The dragons squealed and fled in all directions. The world was ending. Sophie glanced up to see a glowing rock the size of a football pitch heading straight for her.

No!

Gasping, she jolted upright in her bed. Breathing heavily and dripping with sweat, her heart was trying to escape her chest. She looked around her bedroom. There was no water. No creature. No burning rocks. *It was another dream.*

Overwhelmed with thirst, she eased herself out of bed, picked up her glass from the bedside table and wandered along the landing. The floorboards of her terraced house creaked, but not enough to wake mum, whose snoring sounded like a steam train. Deciding not to turn on the garishly bright bathroom light, which was always accompanied by the din of an old extractor fan, she slipped into the bathroom in darkness, filled the glass from the tap and gulped down the refreshing water. Sweat glistened on the forehead of her dimly lit reflection in the bathroom mirror. She splashed water on her face, towelled it off, refilled the glass and returned it to her bedside table.

The pillow was damp, so she turned it over and let her head collapse backwards onto it. Her eyes flicked around her bedroom. It was small and didn't contain much beyond her bed, desk and wardrobe, but it was clean and perfectly organised. Moonlight peaked through the curtains and lit Dad's framed picture, which hung on the opposite wall. Mike Williams smiled warmly back at Sophie.

She reached over for her watch, which was charging on her desk. "Diary," she whispered. The watch projected a display of an old-fashioned diary floating in front of her face. She grabbed her digital pen, flicked onto a fresh page and started writing in mid-air.

Hi Dad,

I've just had the same dream. It's getting more vivid. I could see the creature more clearly under the water this time. The rocks came down, and one almost hit me before I woke up. It was terrifying. I have no idea what it means. I've still not told anyone about it, except you.

Sophie paused and twiddled the pen in her fingers. She stared at the moon peeking through her curtains. The clock in the corner of the projection showed 2:47 am. Realising it was past midnight, a wave of sadness washed through her.

It's Friday 23rd now, which means today is the second anniversary. Two years since, well, I was last with you.

I miss you so much, Daddy.

A tear rolled down her cheek. Her eyelids closed like floodgates holding back a river. She sighed deeply before opening them and continuing.

I'm still trying my best to make a difference, as you told me to. I think people appreciate it. After school today, I served dinners at the homeless centre again, and I think they appreciated it. I know Jackie did, anyway, because she was so short of helpers today. But whatever I do, I never feel like it's enough. I just don't know what to do sometimes.

Anyway, night night daddy.

Love you xx

She put the watch down, rolled onto her side and cried into her pillow.

Later that morning, Sophie felt exhausted after her disturbed night. At least it was Friday – the last school day of the week. She changed her bedsheets, aware the old ones were soaked with a mixture of sweat and tears, showered, put on her school uniform and went downstairs. Her mum, Mari, prepared breakfast in the kitchen.

"Good morning, Sophie, my love," Mari said in her strong Welsh accent. Mari was a short, plump lady who always had a big smile above her double chin. "I'm doing porridge."

The small kitchen/dining room was old fashioned and cluttered. A dresser, which seemed too big for the room, towered over the wooden dining table. Every shelf was overloaded with knickknacks, papers and photos of Sophie, mum and dad, with Sophie at various stages of her childhood. Her mum's red hair and freckly skin contrasted with dad's dark hair and skin, resulting in Sophie's unique look – olive skin tone, brown wavy hair, and freckles. Sophie liked her freckles – they reminded her of the stars when she gazed up into the dark, Welsh sky.

"Morning, mum." Her voice was low and subdued as she pulled out a chair and sat down.

Her mum glanced up from the bowl of porridge she was stirring. "Are you ok, sweetheart? You look terrible."

Mari's assessment of her appearance failed to improve Sophie's mood. "I'm fine," Sophie murmured, without looking up.

Mari left the porridge and sat down next to her daughter. She grabbed Sophie's hands and looked her in the eyes. "Come on, talk to your mother; what is it?"

Sophie looked down into her lap and spoke almost inaudibly. "Bad night. Weird dream, and then I was thinking about dad."

"Oh, darling. It's two years today, isn't it? Shall we go and visit him after school?"

Sophie disliked visiting dad's grave. It made her feel even sadder, but she felt like she should today and wanted to support mum, who liked going. Sophie was all too aware of the grief her mum was still feeling. When mum was at his grave, she spoke to dad there as if he were alive. It was her way of coping.

"Yeah, ok."

The crisp morning air made Sophie feel better as she wandered through the village on her way to school. She noticed a familiar face on the opposite side of the road. "Hi, David!"

David was a thin man with a messy beard and tatty clothes. He walked with a limp and was carrying a bin bag full of his belongings. "Hello, Sophie," he called back in his thick Welsh accent and with a broad grin. "I was so glad the day centre was open last night.

Thank you for my dinner. It is so nice having a warm meal on a cold night!"

"No problem David. Glad you enjoyed it. Take care!"

"You're a good girl Sophie. You have a good day."

The thank you from David gave Sophie a warm feeling inside. As she continued strolling through the village, she spotted a red kite circling gracefully over the frosty branches of oak trees, which were sparkling as the sun bounced off what remained of their leaves. She filled her lungs with the fresh morning air. Suddenly, it felt like it was going to be a good day after all.

The grey school building came into view as Sophie rounded the final bend. Other kids swarmed towards it from all directions, some in small self-driving buses, some on electric scooters of various designs and some on old fashioned pedal bikes. Those who lived further away came by drone, each of which could carry several people. They buzzed in like bees and touched down on the school roof, which had special landing pads and staircases down to the main building. Sophie could have used a driverless bus, but she liked to walk, partly to escape the inane chatter of other children and partly to get fresh air and exercise.

The school corridors were always chaotic. A crowd of kids, most considerably older and taller than Sophie, were running, shouting and making fun of each other.

She tried to ignore the mayhem and marched straight to her classroom. There were several groups of children chatting and laughing in their little cliques.

She had been at secondary school a couple of months now and knew she should make more effort to socialise with her new classmates, but they all seemed to know each other so well. She felt like an outsider. When she did talk to the other kids, she often found the conversation boring and childish, although she felt guilty for feeling that way.

On this particular morning, a group of boys were gathered around a screen talking excitedly. Sophie thought she overheard one of them mention Space Command, which grabbed her attention. Space Command was the global space organisation. The main spaceport was in Wales, not too far from where she lived. She had passed it many times and had stared at the grand entrance gates, wondering what it was like inside. On a clear day, dad would shout when he noticed a rocket climbing into the sky, and they watched together from her bedroom window, something she now did on her own.

She decided to approach the group. "Excuse me, what are you all talking about?"

Josh, a skinny boy with hair that flopped over his glasses, appeared surprised by the question, or maybe he was not used to being approached by a girl. "Space

Command is looking for a child captain for a space mission," he responded nervously whilst showing Sophie the advert on his tablet. The Space Command logo at the top of the screen made it look official.

"Young person with leadership qualities wanted to lead a child-only mission into space. Full training provided. Please apply."

"Even twelve-year-olds can apply," said Josh.

Sophie gasped. "Child only? They want children to go into space without adults?"

"Yep! It says here – Space Command needs to train and then observe the best young astronauts for a routine mission to learn how kids will cope," replied Josh before turning back to his friends. "I hope they give us laser cannons! Maybe I could go and find aliens and start an intergalactic war."

Josh laughed hysterically at his own comment. Sophie raised an eyebrow and backed away from the conversation, but goosebumps were rising all over her arms. Her mind was racing.

The first lesson was English. Mr Galway, a tall, bulky man with a thick beard and glasses, the combination of which left very little of his facial skin showing, was asking questions at the front of the class.

"How do we complete this sentence using the present continuous form of the verb?"

Other children raised their hands. Sophie stared out of the window at the moon, which was still visible in the daylight.

"Sophie?" asked Mr Galway in his deep voice.

Sophie stared at the half-crescent moon and imagined flying close to it in a spaceship with her team of other children. No adults. *Would they really trust children in charge of a spaceship?*

"Sophie? Earth to Sophie! Come in, Sophie."

The other children laughed.

Sophie snapped back to the classroom. "Sorry, I was...what was the question?"

Chapter Two
Application

Sophie continued to think about the advert whilst walking home that afternoon. She knew there must be a tiny chance of being selected to lead the first-ever child space mission, but should she try? *What if this is my chance to do something important? What if this is my chance to make dad proud?*

She quietly let herself into the house. Wandering through the hallway, she overheard mum chatting to Auntie Milly.

"You know, Mill, I'm so worried about Soph. She often seems quiet and disconnected, almost like she's in a dream. She used to be so different. She never seems to have fun with friends like she used to."

The kitchen door was open a crack, just enough for Sophie to peek through. Auntie Milly lived a long way away, but Mari's tablet projected a holographic image of her onto the kitchen chair, so it was like she was there.

"It's going to be hard on her," Milly said, her ghost-like hologram flickering. "She's only just started big school, she's getting close to her teenage years, and with Mike gone, well, you know. It takes time, Mari. It's all a lot of change."

Sophie hated being the topic of gossip between Mum and Auntie, but rather than make a fuss, she pretended not to have heard. Anyway, she was still buzzing from the Space Command opportunity. Putting on a calm face, she strolled in confidently.

"Hi, Mum. Hi, Auntie." Sophie kissed her mum on the cheek.

"Oh, Sophie, I didn't hear you come in. You seem to be in a good mood!"

Sophie smiled. "Yes, I am! What are you two talking about?"

"Oh, I was just telling your mum about a new pair of shoes I bought today," Milly lied.

"Well, I'm just going to change. Mum, we should go and see dad before it gets dark."

Sophie darted up the stairs two at a time and changed as quickly as she could out of her school uniform and into jeans and a hoodie. She sat at her desk and tapped her watch, which beamed an image onto her desk, flicked to the small print of the Space Command advert and started scribbling notes.

The cemetery was a short walk from Sophie's house. The air was chilly, but still, without a breath of wind. The sky had turned blood red in the west with the setting sun. Sophie and her mum sat on their usual bench next to dad's grave.

"Mum, would you say I have leadership qualities?"

Mari raised her eyebrows. "Sophie, are you serious? That's one of the easiest questions you've ever asked me. You know you do, sweetheart. You were captain of just about every school team at your last school. In fact, you've always been a right little bossy boots, even as a toddler. Jackie told me that you pretty much take charge at the homeless centre. And you order me around often enough."

Sophie was not expecting Mum's response to be so forthright. "I don't mean to. I just like to get things done."

"Well, you take after your dad in that way." Mari turned to look at the marble gravestone. "Doesn't she, Mike? I know she doesn't get it from me." She turned back to Sophie. "Why do you ask?"

Sophie hesitated, wondering if it was a good time to show her the advert. Having dad there, at least in spirit, might help. She knew *he* would have wanted her to go for this. She tapped her watch and projected an image of the advert in front of them. "Mum, I think I could do this. I want to apply. What do you think?"

Mari put her reading glasses on. It seemed to take ages for her to read. A frown developed on her forehead and then increased with every sentence read. There was an awkward silence before tears then started rolling down her cheeks.

Sophie quickly tapped again to turn off the projection. "What is it?"

"Oh, it's nothing, darling. Let me think about it, sweetheart."

"Mum, I didn't want to upset you."

"No, it's ok, my love. Can you give me some time with your dad, please?"

"But mum, I..." Sophie's bottom lip started to quiver. She paused and closed her eyes, desperately trying to avoid getting emotional herself, which she knew would hinder her attempt to obtain her mother's approval. Confused and disappointed, Sophie stood up. "Of course, mum, I'll wait by the gate."

Sophie swore to herself as she watched mum from a distance. She was hoping for an immediate and resounding 'yes' from Mari and was angry that she didn't get one. But she also felt guilty for bringing this up on the anniversary of dad's death.

Sophie was unaware of exactly how dad died. The official story suggested an unfortunate accident at work, but she didn't know any details. She knew dad ran his own engineering company. Most of the time, he was working in his large shed at the end of their garden. Dad's shed had always been a mysterious place. It was a concrete outbuilding with no windows, and a thick electricity cable ran along the fence and connected to it. She was never allowed to go in there when he was alive, and the door had remained locked ever since he died. The locks seemed over the top – there were three substantial bolt locks and two deadlocks. Sophie had suggested they clear it out, but mum refused. Whenever Sophie mentioned it, Mari always got so upset. In the end, Sophie gave up asking, but she never stopped wondering.

Mari was kneeling by the headstone, chatting to dad. It was not the typical way she talked to him. She looked angry as if she were accusing him of something.

Eventually, just as Sophie started to shiver in the cold November evening air, mum got up and marched over to her. Despite the cold weather, Mari looked hot and flustered, with eyes still puffy from the tears.

"Mum, I'm sorry, I was only thinking...."

Mari grabbed Sophie by the hand. "Now, Sophie Williams, you listen to me. I know that anything I say won't make any difference, and once you decide to do something, nothing will stop you. But I think you've had a tough couple of years, and it's about time you did something that you want to do. I want you to apply for this opportunity, do you hear me? You go for it, sweetheart."

As they embraced, Sophie looked over at dad's gravestone with a broad smile. "Thanks!" she mouthed.

Sophie woke up early on Saturday morning. The deadline for the Space Command application form was Monday. *What qualities would be needed?* Leadership, ingenuity, courage, calmness under pressure, dedication. She listed every example she could think of where she had shown each and ticked them off one by one. She then wrote each sentence again and again, improving the wording with each attempt.

She looked up at dad's picture. *I wish you were here to help with this!* She considered reading it to mum, but she seemed so upset by the advert. The last thing she needed was mum's emotions right now. She had to stay positive. *Think positive.*

On Monday morning, Sophie got up early and gave her application form one final read. *It's as good as it's going to get.* Her finger hovered over the submit button. She closed her eyes and took a deep breath, about to press the button, before mum knocked on her door and poked her head around.

"Soph, how are you doing with your form?"

Oh, not now, mum, Sophie thought to herself. "Almost ready, I think."

Mum marched into the bedroom cheerfully and sat on Sophie's bed. "Let me hear your answers then."

Sophie didn't want to read her answers, but she knew trying to avoid it would just lead to an argument, so, reluctantly, she started reading. As she read, tears, again, began to roll down mum's face. Sophie noticed mid-sentence and felt a rush of anger.

"Look, mum, if you don't want me to apply, then just say, and I'll forget the whole thing!"

"No, my love, it's not that." Mari pulled out a handkerchief and wiped her eyes before blowing her nose. "I just thought that your answers sound so grown up. So adult and professional. It's making me feel so proud. I told you, you go for this. I'm with you all the way. I'm just starting to wonder what happened to my little girl."

"Oh, mum!" Sophie got up from her desk and joined Mari on the bed to hug her. She finished reading, and

Mari made a couple of suggestions. There were silly mistakes that Sophie missed and further examples of Sophie's experience which she had forgotten. It surprised Sophie how helpful it was to have a fresh pair of eyes on her writing. After another half hour, they both agreed they could improve the responses no further.

"Press the button, Soph," said Mari, with a smile.

"Thank you for your application. You will hear from us soon."

Sophie sighed. It felt like a weight lifted from her shoulders as she hugged Mari tight. She looked up at dad. His smile seemed to have grown in his picture.

Thursday 29ᵗʰ November 2068, 8:14 am

Sophie munched cornflakes at the kitchen table when her watch pinged with a new message. She casually glanced at it and then spotted the Space Command logo at the top, which caused a surge of adrenaline and an intake of breath.

MESSAGE FOR SOPHIE WILLIAMS,

"Dear Sophie,

Thank you for your application for the position of leader of the first child-only mission into space. We are pleased to inform you that you have progressed to the next round of assessments.

There will be further assignments and activities to help us select the right person.

Kind regards,

Dr Millson
Space Command Mission Designer"

Sophie's hands trembled. Her mum had already gone to work, so she had no one to tell.

"Ok, calm down, Soph," she whispered to herself. "There are probably thousands of kids that have made it through the first stage." However, her attempts at reassuring herself failed as thoughts circled through her mind. *But what if I do make it?*

Chapter Three
Hard Work

When Sophie arrived at her classroom later that morning, she tried to forget about Space Command. The chances of being selected had only slightly improved so it was better to keep it to herself for now.

Josh chatted to his friends, Dylan and Adian, as he showed them something on his tablet. Sophie peaked over Josh's shoulder as she passed by and noticed the Space Command logo.

"Hi, Josh. What are you all looking at?"

Josh sighed. "It's the Space Command thing," he replied in a sullen voice. "I applied for the mission, but they don't want me. Look at their response."

"Dear Josh,

Thank you for your application for the position of leader of the first child-only mission into space. We regret to inform you that you have not been selected to proceed to the next round on this occasion, but we appreciate your interest.

Please continue to consider further opportunities with Space Command in the future.

Kind regards,

Dr Millson
Space Command Mission Designer"

"Oh, Josh, sorry to hear that. Well done for applying." Sophie touched Josh on the arm as she spoke, which seemed to make him blush.

"Thanks. I thought it was worth a try. Why are you so interested anyway, Sophie? Are you thinking of applying?"

Sophie thought she heard a snigger from Josh's two friends, which sparked anger deep inside her. Why did they think it was funny for her to consider applying? She didn't want to tell people about her application yet, and she didn't want to make Josh feel bad, but the look of contempt on the faces of Dylan and Adian convinced her otherwise.

"Erm, well, I actually did apply." Sophie's irritation was clear from her reddening cheeks.

"Oh, cool," replied Josh. "So, did you get the same message, or have you not heard yet?"

So now Josh is assuming that I would be unsuccessful!

Sophie tapped her watch and displayed the message on the school desk. As the three boys read it, their eyes widened. The look of sudden admiration was priceless. Josh's mouth fell open as if a weight hung from his chin. "NO WAY! Sophie, you might be going into space!"

Other children started crowding around. Sophie heard the whispers spread. "Sophie's going into space!" Before long, every child from her class had gathered, everyone eager to find out what was happening.

Sophie's anger had turned to embarrassment. Now, her face blushed with all the attention. "It's only the first step. There is still a long way to go."

Questions started coming thick and fast from the sea of faces.

"Where will you be going, Sophie?"

"Will you really be with no adults?"

"Are you just going to the moon, or Mars, or further?"

Sophie felt a thrill she had not experienced before. Never had she been the centre of attention like she was now. Before she had time to attempt answering any questions, Mr Galway came into the classroom to start the English lesson.

"EVERYONE SIT DOWN!" he bellowed. Eventually, the class took their seats. "What was all the commotion about?"

Josh, looking proud, decided to answer on Sophie's behalf. "Sir, Sophie's made it through to the next round of the Space Command opportunity! She might soon be leading a team of kids into space!"

Mr Galway raised his eyebrows and looked at Sophie, whose face was now beetroot red. "Have you really, Sophie?" He paused for an uncomfortably long time. Sophie wasn't sure if he was expecting an answer, and she didn't want to speak in front of the whole class. Fortunately, Mr Galway continued. "Well, congratulations. But for now, we must focus on more down to earth matters. Everyone turn to page 46 of your e-book."

The school bell clanged at the end of the lesson, followed by the usual clamour as everyone rushed to pack their devices away.

Lowri Jones, one of the most popular girls in the class, came over to Sophie's desk before leaving. "Bye, Sophie," she said with a smile.

"Er, bye," replied Sophie, surprised. Lowri had never once spoken to her before that moment.

Josh's friend Dylan tapped Sophie on the shoulder as he strolled past. "See you later, Space Girl!"

Sophie smiled and stared into the middle distance. She tried to decide if she liked the nickname 'Space Girl'. It was so cheesy, but part of her loved it.

"Sophie, could you wait behind please?" shouted Mr Galway, trying to make himself heard over the noise.

Sophie waited for the classroom to empty. Mr Galway approached Sophie with his usual stern look on his face.

"So, Sophie, this Space Command thing...."

Sophie's mind was spinning. Mr Galway seemed to hate anything that took attention away from his English teaching, and she expected a lecture about how she should concentrate on her schoolwork. In his eyes, she was now a significant class distraction, which he needed to control.

"Er, yes, sir. I promise I won't let it interfere with my studies."

To Sophie's surprise, Mr Galway's typical frown switched to a beaming grin as he let out a hearty laugh. "No, Sophie, I'm sure you won't. I know how hardworking you are. No, I just wanted to say well done. I don't tell many people this, but I'm an amateur astronomer myself." He pulled out his old-fashioned phone and showed Sophie a picture of his telescope, which looked out of his garden shed (which he called his observatory), and then proudly ran through dozens of images he had taken of the planets.

"I wish you the very best of luck, Sophie, and let me know if I can help with any of the English in your assignments. I'd be more than happy to look at them before you send them in."

Sophie knew the application process would be tough, but the streams of exams and assessments from Space Command were even more demanding than she imagined. There were essays on how she would respond in situations, memory tests, logic tests, intelligence tests. It was relentless. After the first week, having worked for hours every evening after school, she felt mentally drained. Then she opened a message from Dr Millson, which made her heart sink:

"We need to test the physical fitness of all applicants. You will need to undertake running challenges and submit the results to us."

Running challenges? How can I do running challenges when I'm absolutely exhausted? Thanks to walking to school every day, Sophie was reasonably fit but never considered herself a runner. She liked sports, and although she was not the most gifted, she was often captain due to her ability to organise others and tell them what to do – what her mum would describe as being a 'right little bossy boots'.

December mornings in Wales were cold, dark and wet, but early mornings were her only option as she had no other time available during a typical school day, so she set her alarm for six the following morning. She found her trainers, tracksuit bottoms and hoody and placed them neatly next to her bed, ready for the morning. *Make this new running habit as easy as possible,* she thought.

The following morning, however, was anything but easy. The alarm seemed to have increased in volume since last night. With her eyes closed, Sophie missed three times before banging the off button. She then forced her eyes open and checked the outside temperature on her watch. Minus five degrees. *That's the same temperature as the freezer!* The bed felt so warm and cosy. She considered abandoning the run and trying again tomorrow when it might be warmer, but then she looked at dad. She briefly fantasised about becoming the first-ever kid in space, something she found herself doing alarmingly often. *Okay, Soph. You've got this. Count down from five, and before you get to one, be out of bed. Five, four, three, two...*

She was up. Before she had a chance to experience second thoughts, she put her running gear on and headed downstairs and out into the crisp winter morning. Frost sparkled on the ground under the streetlights. Stars twinkled in the sky, and the full moon looked huge.

She tried to jog to the park, just a few hundred metres from her house, but the icy pavements were treacherous, so she slowed to a walk. The warm water droplets from her breath instantly condensed into misty clouds as they left her mouth. The park was dark, but the combination of moonlight and the small number of streetlights was enough for her to see. She lifted her watch to her mouth.

"Record run," she instructed.

"Recording. Enjoy your run," came the reply in an overly enthusiastic American accent.

How does anyone enjoy running in a freezer? The grass crunched underfoot. The cold air hurt her lungs as she started to put one foot in front of the other. The taste of sick travelled up from her stomach as she burped, but she managed to hold it in and continue. It was painful, but at least she was doing it.

After half a lap of the park, which seemed to go on forever, the American man's voice from her watch told her she had completed 500 metres. Her target was three kilometres, but her legs were already aching, her lungs were stinging, and she felt ever closer to throwing up. *Soph, it's only running. It won't kill you. Just keep going.*

She tried to let her mind go blank and forget about the distance. Her rhythm improved as she settled into a comfortable pace. After two kilometres, she felt better, partly because there was just one lap to go and partly because her body had warmed up.

The last kilometre was a struggle. Every part of Sophie's body seemed to be screaming, 'STOP RUNNING'. In her mind's eye, she repeatedly flicked between images of Space Command and her dad, the combination of which forced her to continue.

The final 500 metres were torture. Maybe she had started too quick, considering it was her first run. *Come on, Sophie, what are you made of? Don't slow down now. Run faster.* She abandoned Space Command and her dad and imagined a crowd cheering her as if she were at the Olympics. *Sophie Williams is leading the 3,000 metres to bring gold home for Wales. What a fantastic run by the young girl. The crowd here in Cardiff are going crazy.* She started quickening her steps and pumping her arms and legs. For the last 100 metres, she found herself in a flat-out sprint finish against imaginary competitors.

"Distance: Three kilometres," announced the man on her watch.

Gasping for breath, Sophie collapsed out-stretched onto the frozen grass, which now felt pleasantly cool. As the pain subsided and her accelerated heart rate started returning to normal, the rush of endorphins in her brain made her feel on top of the world. She stared up at the blanket of stars as if she were in a trance. They looked beautiful. *Perhaps I can get used to running.*

After school that day, Sophie tucked into vegetable lasagne at the kitchen table with her mum when another ping came from her watch. It was from Space Command again.

Mari shook her head. "Won't these people ever leave you alone?"

Sophie could not resist reading it.

"Dear Sophie,

We are sending you equipment to enable you to participate in group activities. It will be delivered to your house shortly.

Kind regards,

Dr Millson
Space Command Mission Designer"

Moments later, a small helicopter drone carrying a box gently descended in their back garden, landing just in front of dad's shed. When the box was just a few millimetres from the concrete path, the drone released the cargo and lifted quickly into the sky and out of view.

Mari smiled at Sophie. "Oooh! Now they're sending you presents."

Sophie rushed down the last of her lasagne, ran outside to grab the package, brought it in and put it on the kitchen table. After wrestling through multiple layers of bubble wrap, she eventually found a pair of the latest virtual reality glasses.

Usually, Sophie would help tidy up the kitchen after dinner, but she looked at Mari with her puppy dog eyes and a big smile. No words were necessary.

"Go on, go and play with your new toy," said Mari.

Sophie sprinted up the stairs, sat at her desk and emptied the contents of the parcel. There were two black gloves at the bottom, which she almost overlooked amongst the packaging. She slid her hands into the gloves, put the glasses on and pressed the power button on the side. Everything beeped into life, and the view of her bedroom wall faded to black. After a brief pause, writing appeared in front of her. It was read aloud in a female British accent.

"Acquiring data for your avatar – please wait."

Seconds later, a digital version of herself appeared. The likeness was remarkable. It even showed Sophie's freckles, which covered her nose and cheeks.

"Are you happy with your avatar?"

"Yes," Sophie replied.

The glasses transported Sophie into a bright, white space. Ahead of her was the Space Command logo. It slid open, and a lady with frizzy ginger hair and glasses marched through the opening and approached her.

"Hello Sophie, I'm Dr Millson. Congratulations on getting to this stage of the application process."

Chapter Four
First Exercise

Sophie gasped when confronted by the avatar of Dr Millson. "Thank you, Dr Millson, it's nice to, er, meet you," she replied, unsure if this counted as meeting someone.

"I'm sure you have many questions, but this is a recording, so I can't answer them now. I just wanted to introduce you to the Space Command Virtual Training Arena."

Sophie smiled and shook her head. It was a pre-recorded message. She felt silly for talking to it as if it was live.

"You will be taking part in group activities here with fellow applicants. We will be watching to see how you work together as a team. Would you like to start an activity now?"

Sophie tried to decide if she felt ready for an exercise. She was unprepared, but what preparation could she do? If she didn't do it now, she knew she would lie awake all night thinking about it.

"Yes."

Dr Millson's avatar glitched while it loaded the next recording. "Excellent. On walking through the door, you will be placed in a team of six. Please enter now."

In real life, hairs on Sophie's arms stood on end in anticipation. She was about to meet fellow applicants. The Space Command logo door slid open. By pointing both of her index fingers forwards, she moved her avatar through it and emerged on the control deck of a spaceship. Her eyes widened as she glanced around. Everything looked incredibly real. Touchscreen control panels were integrated into beige wall and desk units. There were padded swivel chairs in various positions and a display screen covering the front of the room.

Before Sophie had time to appreciate her new surroundings, the door slid open again, and through it wandered the avatar of a slim boy with dark skin and a mass of floppy black hair. His avatar smiled broadly as soon as he saw Sophie.

"Hello. My name is Sahil Mukherjee. It's very nice to meet you."

Sophie recognised the name and the face, but she was trying to recall how. It suddenly twigged. "Sahil? Are you the genius scientist from India? I read about you in Science Monthly. You've won prizes for new scientific theories?"

Sahil's avatar blushed. "Yes, I did, although I've been quite lucky and had lots of help. But yes, I have always been fascinated by science, and I want to understand how the universe works. My uncle is a famous scientist and a professor at the Indian Institute of Science in Bangalore, and he helped me with much of my work. I am applying for the role of Mission Scientist. I very much hope I get to go to space. This is so exciting! I'm sorry, what is your name and where do you live, and which position are you applying for?"

"Sophie Williams, Wales, I'm applying to lead the mission."

"Oh, wow, that's a big responsibility. Very best of luck to you, Sophie."

Sophie instantly liked Sahil. Even via his avatar, he came across as humble and kind. She noticed he talked a lot, sometimes a bit too much, with eyes as wide as dinner plates and enthusiasm that was infectious. She wondered how he managed to breathe between sentences.

Eventually, one by one, four other children entered the room. A girl called Ling from China, and two boys; Femi from Egypt and Emil from Germany. The three of them were also all applying to be the leader. Sophie couldn't help feeling threatened as they seemed so intelligent and confident. By far the most confident was a boy named Jack, who came into the room last. He had dark skin, neatly trimmed black hair and a huge smile.

"Hey, all! I'm Jack from Michigan, USA. I'm the master engineer."

Why would anyone describe themself as a master engineer when they are only twelve, thought Sophie.

Dr Millson's voice was broadcast over the loudspeaker, which interrupted the conversations. "Your group exercise will start shortly. In this scenario, you are travelling on one of our newest star ships, Flourish. Your mission is to prepare for an emergency landing on Earth by safely manoeuvring the ship into Earth's atmosphere. To complete the mission, you must land as soon as possible. Good luck."

An image of Earth appeared across the entire front screen of the control deck. The planet was growing in size by the second.

A computerised voice made an announcement. "Approaching Earth's atmosphere in five minutes. Warning – engines 2 and 4 are offline."

The six children stared at each other.

"Are you kidding?" shouted Jack in his American accent.

"We need to decide who is in charge," said Femi. "I think I should be because I'm applying for the captain's position."

"I'm applying for captain as well," said Emil in his German accent.

Sophie felt a flash of anger. "Guys, we don't have time to argue about this. Let's just decide between us who does what. Jack, you're the engineer. Find out what is wrong with engines 2 and 4."

"Yes, ma'am!" Jack scooted across to a touchscreen display and started tapping buttons.

"We don't have a pilot," Sophie said. "Does anyone here have any piloting experience?"

The children all looked at each other sheepishly.

"Ok, I assume that's a no. I am no pilot, but I have studied how the controls work. I can have a go unless there are any objections?"

"Fine with me!" replied Femi, and murmurs of agreement came from Ling and Emil.

Sophie moved into the pilot's chair at the front of the control deck and started tapping buttons, trying to remember what does what.

Meanwhile, Sahil was studying one of the control panels. "Sophie, we need to reduce velocity urgently.

At this speed, we will disintegrate in Earth's atmosphere in, er, approximately 36 seconds."

In real life, Sophie felt sweat dripping from her forehead and around her virtual reality glasses. In the virtual world, she was tapping furiously at her screen. "Ok, I'm trying to find the reverse rocket boost. This is slightly different to what I studied."

Femi wanted to look like he was doing something. "Ling, Emil, can you help Sophie to find the, er, deceleration button?"

Ling and Emil looked over Sophie's shoulder.

"I think it could be this?" said Emil nervously.

Sophie tapped the button, which allocated the joystick to the main thrust controls. "Yes – thanks!" She then eased the joystick towards her.

"That's good. We're slowing down," said Sahil, "but it's not enough. We need to slow down more, or we will burn up like a, er, like a piece of toast that has been cooked too long. My brother always burns toast like this."

Sophie glanced at Sahil, amazed that he felt he had time to talk about his brother's cooking issues. She then snapped back to the job at hand. "Jack, I need more power! What's happening with those other engines?"

"The rockets went down because they overheated. I'm doing a full restart, but it's going to take more time."

The control deck started to shake and vibrate.

"How long?" shouted Femi.

"Another few minutes."

Sophie wrestled with the joystick to try to slow the ship more. "That's too long!"

"You must make it quicker, Jack!" instructed Emil, trying to look like he was taking charge.

"Hey, if you know how to speed this up, then you come and sit here and take over!"

We're not going to make it, thought Sophie. She turned to face the others. "We need to abandon the approach. We're going to die if we continue. We need to go back up into space!"

"But the mission said we must land as soon as possible," said Ling. "If we ascend now, we will ruin our approach."

"Surely, it's better to survive and save ourselves and the ship rather than try to follow orders and die?"

The kids looked at each other in silence. No one wanted to be the one to make the decision.

"Sorry to interrupt," said Sahil, "we have 20 seconds before we are my brother's toast."

"Are there any objections to abandoning the mission?" shouted Sophie.

Silence.

"Okay, then." She turned to face the controls, pushed a joystick with her left hand, which increased the forward thrust, and pulled another joystick with her right hand to fire auxiliary rockets. On the screen, the Earth began to descend and was soon replaced with a view of stars.

"Landing approach abandoned," announced the ship.

Suddenly, from Sophie's perspective, everyone and everything paused as if time froze. Writing appeared in front of her face, accompanied by the same female British voice which asked her if she liked her Avatar.

"Mission failed. End of scenario. Thank you for your participation in this Space Command group exercise."

Sophie was back at her desk in her small bedroom. She pulled off the glasses and gloves, threw them on the desk and stared at the wall. *Mission failed? But what else could we have done?* The events of the exercise raced through her mind again and again. *Mission failed.*

She was angry at her teammates for not being more helpful and at herself for not knowing how to take the ship safely into the atmosphere. Should she have studied even more? Suddenly, the whole thing felt like a waste of time.

Staring at her bedroom ceiling until two in the morning, Sophie desperately tried to think of something positive, but all she kept seeing was those words. *Mission failed.*

The following day, Sophie woke up groggily and barely uttered a word over breakfast with mum. The walk to school did nothing to lift her mood. What started as drizzle deteriorated into torrential rain. The bottom of her tights became sodden as she trudged through ankle-deep puddles, and then a self-driving bus sped straight through a huge puddle and drenched the rest of her.

"Hey, Space Girl!" said Josh cheerily as Sophie entered the classroom. "How's the star trek training going?"

"Oh, shut up, Josh," responded Sophie. Josh's face fell as she marched past him and sat at her desk. Mr Galway was at the front of the class, peering at her disapprovingly over the top of his glasses. *Oh, great! Now, I'm probably going to get into trouble.*

The day crawled at a snail's pace, during which Sophie tried to avoid talking to anyone. All she could think about was that she had messed up her one chance to do something meaningful with her life. *Her one chance to make dad proud.*

To make matters worse, the rest of her classmates seemed annoyingly cheerful, except for Josh, who appeared as depressed as she was. Josh's sad expression made her feel even worse. He was probably the closest thing she had to a friend at this new school. He kept glancing over at her, but Sophie just avoided eye contact.

When the bell eventually rang, Mr Galway called for Sophie to stay behind. "Oh no," groaned Sophie quietly. All she wanted to do was get to her bedroom, close the door and collapse onto her bed.

Mr Galway remained at his desk as Sophie approached. "Sophie, you don't seem quite yourself today. Is everything okay?"

"Sorry, sir. I was soaking wet this morning, and I wasn't really in the mood for...." Sophie's voice trailed off as she thought about the real reason. She decided to be honest. "I think I've messed it up."

Sophie explained everything that happened during the virtual mission. Mr Galway listened intently and then paused for a minute, took off his glasses and leaned back in his chair. "Sophie, you don't know if you've failed. You may still have an excellent chance."

"I keep trying to tell myself that, but I just don't believe it. I can't help feeling angry. Or maybe it's stupid to think someone like me could ever go into space, let alone lead a mission."

A tear rolled down Sophie's cheek. She wiped it away, sniffed and apologised.

"Don't apologise, Sophie." My Galway appeared thoughtful. "Have you ever heard of a lady named Amy Carmichael?"

What is he talking about? Just let me go home!

"No, sir, I haven't."

"Amy was an Irish lady, who helped a great many girls in India; girls that would have otherwise experienced extreme suffering."

Sophie started to feel guilty for her earlier thoughts.

"She was also a writer, and there is a quote I always like to keep with me."

My Galway pulled an old book from the top drawer of his desk and started flicking through the worn pages. "Ah, here it is."

"Let us not be surprised when we have to face difficulties. When the wind blows hard on a tree, the roots stretch and grow the stronger, let it be so with us. Let us not be weaklings, yielding to every wind that blows, but strong in spirit to resist."

Those words were like a wake up call the sent shivers down Sophie's spine. *I need to be strong in spirit. Difficult things will only make me stronger.* It was the kind of thing her dad used to say.

I need to stop feeling sorry for myself. I need to be a leader. I need to put everything I have into the rest of this application.

"Thank you, sir. Sorry, I've got to go." Without waiting for permission, Sophie ran out of the classroom, sprinted along the corridor, out the school and to the line of kids waiting for driverless buses. Josh was at the front, about to board one. "Josh, wait!"

To Josh's amazement, Sophie ran up to him, opened her arms and hugged him. Other boys in the line started mocking, with wolf-whistles and chants of "Josh has got a girlfriend!" Sophie didn't care.

"Sophie, wh-what are you doing?" asked Josh, mid hug.

Sophie broke off the hug and looked him in the eyes. "I'm sorry for being rude to you this morning. I didn't do very well at one of the Space Command exercises last night, but I've decided I'm going to try even harder."

Josh's face was bright pink. "Well, I could always, er, h-help you study, maybe, sometime?"

Sophie grinned. "I'd like that."

There were plenty more group exercises, assessments, running challenges and essays thrown at Sophie over the following months. Josh came over every couple of weeks, and it was helpful having a study partner. He seemed as determined for Sophie to succeed as she was and took on the role of examiner—testing Sophie on what she needed to remember.

Even on Christmas morning, Sophie was buried deep into one of her holographic books. This one was about rocket engines. Mum poked her head around the bedroom door and listened to Sophie mumbling to herself.

"TVC system? What the heck is a TVC system? Why do they always talk in letters? Oh, Thrust Vector Control. Ok, what is that?"

"Sophie, darling, sorry to interrupt, I just wanted to say Merry Christmas! Don't you want to give yourself a break, on today of all days? Your cousins will be arriving soon with Auntie Milly."

"Sorry mum, Merry Christmas. You were asleep, so I just decided to do a bit of revision before you woke up. I must have got carried away. I'll be down soon."

Thursday 21st February 2069, 8:27 pm

Almost three months had passed since Sophie first applied for the space mission, and the strain on her was taking its toll. That February evening, she had fallen asleep at her bedroom desk with a holographic video playing on loop. The video was describing how pneumatic cargo bay doors on the latest spaceships open and close, and somehow her brain had incorporated it into her sleep. She dreamt of being locked outside a spaceship and was unable to open the door to get back in. She was starting to panic when, suddenly, she was transported underwater. The reptile creature with yellow eyes was in front of her again.

"Who are you?"

"Sophie, come quickly."

She knew what was about to happen. The falling rocks. The destruction. She didn't want to see it again and turned away from the creature, swimming in the opposite direction. Something pinged to her left. She turned and tried to swim towards it.

Waking up startled, Sophie realised the ping was a message arriving on her watch. It was from Space Command. She let out a sigh and held the top of her head in her hands. *What do I have to do now?* She wiped some sleepy dust from her left eye and opened the message.

"Dear Sophie,

Congratulations.

You have been selected to lead the first child mission into space.

Please report to Space Command at 0830 hours, Monday 25th February 2069, for your first mission briefing.

Find attached a list of items to bring with you and instructions on how to find us.

Kind regards,

Dr Millson
Space Command Mission Designer"

Sophie blinked and reread it. And again, to make sure she wasn't still dreaming.

"MUM!"

"Just a minute, Soph, I'm sorting the washing."

"MUM, COME HERE, NOW!"

Mari abandoned the pile of laundry and rushed up the stairs. She was out of breath as she came into Sophie's room.

"What is it? What's the matter?"

"Mum, read this!"

Mari scrambled to find her glasses from her pocket and put them on. "Oh! Sophie! Oh, my goodness! Oh, Sophie, well done!"

They hugged tight. Sophie looked up over mum's shoulder at dad. Tears started flowing down her cheeks, which erupted into uncontrollable sobbing.

They broke off the hug, and her mum looked at her, holding her shoulders. "Soph, are you ok?"

"I'm just happy," blubbered Sophie, smiling through the mess of snot and tears. Hearing those words set her mum off too. The two of them continued to cry together.

Chapter Five
Commute

Friday 22nd February 2069, 8:46 am

The next day, Sophie strolled into her classroom feeling on top of the world. Josh, Dylan and Adian were sat around Josh's desk, each staring at a tablet and looking bored.

"Hi guys," Sophie said with a grin.

Dylon responded without looking up from his tablet. "What's up, Space Girl?"

"I will be soon!" Sophie projected her watch display onto the desk.

The boys read the message. Dylon swore at the top of his voice. Adian stared at her, open-mouthed and shaking his head. Josh jumped up and gave Sophie a somewhat awkward hug. He still wasn't used to hugging girls, but the excitement must have got the better of him. Sophie tried to accept the hug as naturally as she could.

"You did it, Sophie! I can't believe you did it. You're actually going."

"You were a massive help, Josh. Thank you."

As before, Sophie's classmates gathered around, and their reactions were overwhelming. She lost count of the number of times she heard, "Oh my god, Sophie!" Even older kids were poking their heads into the classroom and asking what was going on. When they found out, they came in to join the party. Mr Galway looked especially pleased when he discovered the news. He had never smiled so much during an English lesson, which felt less like a lesson and more like a celebration.

At the end of the lesson, Mr Galway approached Sophie and reverted to his typically stern face for a moment. "You will need to be off school on Monday, which requires Headteacher permission. I suggest you go straight to Mrs Jenkins' office to ask."

It was the first time Sophie had been to the Headteacher's office, and she had never spoken to Mrs Jenkins before. She heard rumours that she was strict and hated children missing school. She knocked on the solid oak door and waited outside, biting her fingernails.

"Come in!" came the call.

Sophie pushed the thick door, which failed to budge before realising she had to turn the handle and push simultaneously. Mrs Jenkins sat behind an old-fashioned mahogany desk with exaggerated, heavy curves. Her wiry hair was tied so tightly it looked like it was stretching her forehead. She glanced at Sophie briefly before returning to signing papers. "Don't just stand there; come and sit down."

Sophie sat on the leather-padded chair. The room smelled musty, like old woolly sweaters. "Er, my name is..."

"Just a moment." Mrs Jenkins had the authoritative demeanour of someone that had been in charge for a long time and was used to people doing exactly as she expected. Sophie glanced around the office to pass the time, but she just wanted to get on with asking for permission. The only sound was an old clock ticking loudly, which seemed to make time pass even more slowly.

Eventually, Mrs Jenkins looked up at Sophie over her glasses, which perched on her nose. "Now, what can I do for you, young lady?"

"My name is Sophie Williams. I need to ask permission to...."

Mrs Jenkins' expressionless face transformed into a beaming smile. "Ah! Sophie, I've already received a call from a nice lady called Dr Millson from Space Command. She has explained everything. On behalf of the whole school, congratulations. It's truly remarkable, and it made my morning. Well done. I wish you all the luck in the world!" She paused for a moment with a slightly confused look. "Or whichever world you're going to!"

Monday 25th February 2069, 5:11 am

Sophie woke up with the excitement of a toddler on Christmas morning. She instantly remembered what day it was. *Space Command day!*

Her insides felt like jelly. Although it was early, it was pointless trying to sleep more, so she slipped into her bunny slippers and dressing gown and crept downstairs, or at least tried to creep, but the stairs creaked so much it was a waste of time.

The message from Dr Millson said she needed to arrive at Space Command at 8:30. She tapped her watch. "How long will it take to drive to Space Command from here?"

"In current traffic conditions, your journey will take 58 minutes."

Ok, I'll aim to arrive 45 minutes early. "Book a taxi to arrive here at 6:45 am."

"Your taxi will be arriving at 6:45 am at your current location."

She poured out a bowl of cereal, drenched it with milk and looked again at the 'list of things to bring' that accompanied the message. They had asked for an overnight bag with spare clothes for five days. Sophie had prepared her bag meticulously the night before.

After breakfast, she ran upstairs, showered, brushed her teeth, dried her hair, brushed her hair, got dressed, checked her bag and then sat on her bed. She looked at the clock. 5:47 am—still loads of time.

She decided to wake mum. Her door squeaked as she eased it open. "Mum? Are you awake?"

The answer came with a series of snores and gargles.

"Mum!"

Her mum sat up with panicked eyes and dribble escaping from the corner of her mouth. "Sophie, what is it? What's wrong?"

"Nothing, mum, sorry. I just thought it was time to get ready."

"Oh, you've got your big day. Sorry my love, I..." Mari glanced at her alarm clock. "Hang on; it's still early!"

When the time did finally roll around to 6:45, a self-driving taxi glided up to their house. Sophie held her watch near the sensor on the yellow door, which slid open, and Sophie and her mum got in. The taxi had two grey leather bench seats facing each other. Sophie and Mari sat next to each other on the forwards-facing one. "Where would you like to go today?" asked the computerised voice from the taxi.

"Space Command please," said Sophie with a smile, hardly believing what she was saying.

"Please fasten your seatbelt. Your journey will take approximately one hour."

The taxi drove itself out of the village and merged onto the highway. Sophie fiddled with the taxi's entertainment system, trying to find something to take her mind off things. After flicking through countless TV, movie and gaming options, she decided she just wanted music.

"So, how long might you be away for?"

"Mum, you've asked me that one hundred times already. I don't know. They haven't told us any details yet, only that it will involve children going to space. All I know is that I needed this overnight bag, so I suppose we might be staying over for the next few nights."

"And did they tell you exactly where you will be going yet?"

"No, I don't know. Please, mum, just try to relax. We'll find out soon."

The taxi's central console lit up as it spoke. "There is an obstruction and reports of heavy traffic on your route. You are still on the fastest route. Your arrival time is estimated at 8:35 am."

Sophie's heart sank. Five minutes late. She hated the idea of being late, even if it were only five minutes. It would make such a bad impression.

The traffic on the motorway started to slow before eventually reaching a standstill. Sophie's stress levels were rising. Would they even still want her as a leader if she can't even get to her first appointment on time? She considered sending a message to Space Command, but she decided first to see how bad the traffic was.

Gazing out of the window, a face in another taxi looked vaguely familiar. It was a dark-skinned boy with floppy black hair, approximately Sophie's age. He was alone and looking increasingly agitated. He turned his face towards Sophie's taxi. *It's Sahil! I recognise him from his avatar!*

"Mum, that boy is a genius scientist from India! He's won loads of prizes for developing new scientific theories even though he's only twelve."

"That's nice, dear. Is he at your school?" replied Mari, distracted by the soap opera on her tablet.

"No, mum, he's from India. He was in my group exercises. He must be here for the mission!"

Sahil's taxi crept a few metres ahead. Sophie opened a drawing program on her watch and started scribbling. As her taxi caught up, she banged the glass and projected it onto the window.

Sahil – is that you? Are you on the space mission? It's me, Sophie.

Sahil looked shocked at first and then read the message. His face exploded into a wide toothy grin as he nodded and gave a double thumbs up.

Sophie then wrote again on her display.

If we ever get there!

The two taxis took turns to slowly overtake each other over the next 38 minutes, during which they moved less than 6 kilometres. *I could run there faster than this,* thought Sophie.

Eventually, they got to the source of the gridlock. A vehicle was broken down in the middle of two lanes, blocking both. As they approached, Sophie noticed two boys. An elder boy was directing traffic around their broken-down vehicle, and a younger boy was working under the bonnet.

"What are those idiots doing?" said Sophie.

The younger boy surfaced from his bonnet as he shouted something at the elder boy. Sophie was shocked to discover she recognised him as well.

"Oh my god! It's Jack. Taxi, pull over!"

The computerised voice of the taxi responded. "We cannot pullover on a live motorway unless this is an emergency. Is this an emergency?"

"YES!" shouted Sophie.

"Sophie, what are you doing?" asked Mari. "You're already going to be late. You don't have time to help these people."

"Mum, he also needs to get to Space Command!"

The taxi glided over onto the hard shoulder. Sahil's taxi pulled in behind them. Sophie yanked the door release handle, which had 'Emergency Use Only' in large red letters just above it, and darted amongst the almost stationary traffic to the broken-down car.

The boy had his head under the bonnet and was repeatedly swearing in an American accent.

"Jack?"

Jack banged his head on the underside of the bonnet. He swore again before standing up straight to see who it was that had startled him.

"Oh! Sophie? You look so much like your avatar!"

"Jack, what are you doing?"

"This is my brother's car. He's studying here, so I came over from Michigan and stayed at his place last night, and he offered me a ride to Space Command, but the stupid thing is a piece of junk. I thought I could fix it!"

"So, the reason the mission scientist, engineer and captain are going to be late for the first mission briefing is due to the engineer being unable to repair his brother's car?" said Sophie, a smirk creeping across her face.

Jack raised one eyebrow. "Wait, who is the mission scientist?"

"Sahil is in the other taxi."

"Oh, cool, I love that guy!"

Sahil approached the other two, nervously trying to avoid slow-moving cars. "Hello, Jack. May I ask why you are trying to fix a car in the middle of a motorway?"

Jack repeated the story, which sounded even more ridiculous the second time.

"Well, we could all take one taxi from here," suggested Sahil, "but we will still be very late. We have 15 minutes to get there, and there is more traffic ahead. The journey is still 45 minutes. I very much didn't want to be late for our first meeting."

"Look, I'm sorry, ok! It was a dumb idea to try to fix this thing, but blame my brother for buying it in the first place!"

Sophie thought for a moment. She also hated the idea of Dr Millson standing around waiting for them. She looked down the motorway. The traffic was speeding up but then slowing down again in the distance. She then glanced upwards, and a thought came to her. "Let's call a drone!"

"Oh, yeah!" said Jack, wiping his hands on his jeans. "You guys have drone taxis in Wales?"

"Yes, we have drone taxis," replied Sophie sarcastically and looking irritated by the question. She tapped her watch and ordered the drone. "It will be here in less than five minutes. I'll also call a repair company to come and fix your brother's car. Sahil, you can send your taxi away, and I'll go and say goodbye to my mum."

Sophie suddenly noticed how easily she took charge of things and didn't want to appear overly bossy straight away. "If that's ok with you two?" she added.

"Yeah, I suppose that makes sense," replied Jack. "But I'll send you some money for the drone as it's kind of my fault."

Sophie got back into her taxi to explain the situation to Mari.

"Are you sure you don't want me to come with you in the helicopter?" asked Mari.

It always amused Sophie how she still called them helicopters. "No, I'm okay, mum. If I'm going to space alone, I think I can handle a short trip to Space Command."

"Plus, you want to be with your new friends, I suppose. Ok, well, call me as soon as you can."

Mari adapted the route on her taxi so it would turn around at the next junction. Sophie gave her a hug, got out and watched her taxi drive off into the traffic. Sahil released his taxi, which drove away in search of a new job. Jack told his brother what was happening, who looked relieved with the new plan.

A few moments later, the sleek, silver drone swooped over the trees to the side of the highway using its short wings before switching to propellers to hover and touch down on the verge. The three of them clamoured over the crash barrier, got inside and buckled up. The black and red trim of the interior reminded Sophie of a sports car. It lifted effortlessly into the air and zoomed along the motorway route, passing over Mari's taxi within seconds.

As they raced over the Welsh landscape, Sophie started to feel heavy-hearted. She remembered the last time she took a drone – a special trip to the beach on her ninth birthday. Dad instructed the drone to continue beyond the landing pads, over the beach and out over the sea, hovering just a few metres. "I'm going straight for a swim," he said as he forced the door open, overriding the safety controls. "See you on the beach!"

"Mike, don't be an idiot!" shouted Mari, but it was too late. Dad had whipped his t-shirt off and dived in.

Later, on the beach, Sophie asked him why he did it. "Wasn't it a bit risky, dad? You could have hurt yourself."

"Sophie, sometimes you need to push yourself and take a few risks. It makes life more interesting."

Sahil was chatting enthusiastically with Jack but paused when he noticed Sophie's expression. "Are you ok, Sophie?"

Sophie blinked, looked at Sahil and smiled. "Yeah, I'm good. This is going to be exciting."

The Space Command complex came into view on the horizon. As they got closer, the children stared in amazement. Grey industrial buildings covered half the site, and the other half was a parking lot of huge rocket ships on stands. Vehicles buzzed in all directions, some travelling on the road, some on rails, some in the air.

For a moment, the taxi hovered a few metres from the main gate, outside of the large metal fence which secured the site. A message appeared on the screen of the taxi. "Welcome, Sophie. This is Space Command security. We have verified your identity. Your airborne taxi will proceed to main reception."

The taxi flew over the fence and approached a tall, glass building. The Space Command logo glistened above the main entrance. It touched down in a dedicated landing zone right outside the front door. The three children hopped out and watched their empty taxi take off. Sophie looked up at the size of the building towering over her. Everything looked enormous. The butterflies were back in her tummy. She took a deep breath. *This is my big chance.*

Chapter Six
Briefing

The glass doors slid open. Sophie, Jack and Sahil wandered into a vast reception area. There were pictures of famous astronauts on the walls, parts of rockets from previous missions on display and large models of planets and star systems. A large portrait of Professor Yang, Director of Space Command, hung above the reception desk. Sophie had read all about him. He was the first human to walk on Mars and had been to many distant stars.

The place was buzzing with activity. Streams of people were going in and out, and many more were standing around or sitting on leather sofas, chatting.

Sahil's eyes had grown even wider. "Oh my goodness! I cannot tell you how excited I am feeling right now."

"You and me, both!" said Jack.

Three receptionists sat behind a long, gleaming desk, bathed in blue light. They all looked extremely busy.

"I'll tell them we're here," said Sophie.

None of the receptionists noticed Sophie. She tried coughing on purpose, but still, they didn't see her. "Hello," she said quietly. Still no reaction. *Did they not hear me, or are they ignoring me?*

Come on, Soph. You've earned your right to be here. Be confident.

"Good morning!" she almost shouted cheerfully.

The middle-aged man lifted his head and looked surprised. "How can I help you, young lady?"

"My name is Sophie Williams. I'm here for the, er..." she was going to say children's mission to space, but it sounded ridiculous in her mind, so she changed the wording, "to meet with Dr Millson."

The man smiled broadly. "Welcome, Sophie. I'll let Dr Millson know you're here."

"Thanks. Sahil and Jack are here, too."

"Well, that makes four of you then. There's another visitor here for the same meeting. She's just over there. You can join her if you like."

Sophie looked over to where the man was pointing. A short, slim girl with pale skin, torn jeans, a purple T-shirt and bright green trainers was perched on the front edge of a leather sofa. She was reading the Space Command official newsletter, copies of which were placed on all the coffee tables.

Sophie wandered over. "Hi, I'm Sophie. Are you on the mission?"

"Er, hi," the girl said in a soft, Scandinavian accent. "Yes." She stood and started to put her hand out for Sophie to shake and then withdrew it, as if aware it's not the kind of thing kids do, so instead resorted to biting her fingernails.

Sophie felt relieved she wasn't the only one showing signs of nerves. She tried to make the girl feel better by putting her hand out. "It's ok. We can shake hands! I suppose we have to pretend to be more like adults now! What's your name?"

The girl accepted the handshake, but it still felt awkward. "Leena."

Jack and Sahil were looking at the displays of space memorabilia and chatting enthusiastically. Sophie suspected it had turned into a competition about who knew more about space stuff.

"Jack, Sahil, come over here!" Sophie shouted across the room. "Meet Leena. She's also on the mission. Leena, Jack will be our engineer, and Sahil is the scientist."

"Hey Leena," said Jack with a grin.

"Hello Leena, it is a pleasure to meet you," said Sahil smoothly. He put his hand out, and Leena shook it more naturally this time.

"So, Leena, tell us a bit about you," Sophie said.

"I'm the pilot."

Sophie was surprised by how little Leena spoke. "Cool. Where are you from, and how did you make it onto the mission."

"To be honest, I can't believe I was selected. I grew up in a small town in Finland and learnt to fly aeroplanes when I was a toddler on my parents' laps. They said I beat thousands of children in the flying simulator contests, which is why I was chosen for the mission." Leena's eyes glanced side to side as she spoke as if direct eye contact would be painful. "I don't know why, but I've always been good at controlling machines."

"I was obsessed with building rockets," said Jack, clearly wanting to bring the conversation back to himself. "When I was six, I got in trouble when one rocket I built went much higher than I expected, and they said it was a danger to commercial aircraft. I also loved inventing things. I once built a robot with my best friend Jess that tried to tidy children's bedrooms. It was pretty good, but it couldn't get the hang of pairing socks!"

A tall lady with frizzy ginger hair and small glasses approached them. Sophie instantly recognised her. "Sophie, Sahil, Jack and Leena? Welcome to Space Command. I'm Dr Millson. Thank you for getting here on time. We have a room full of people waiting to meet you. I heard there was trouble on the motorway?"

Jack gave Sophie and Sahil a wide-eyed look as if to say, "don't you dare tell her what caused the trouble". Sophie struggled not to laugh.

"Well, children," continued Dr Millson, "are you ready to find out more about your adventure?"

The four children couldn't help gawping in all directions as Dr Millson led them through the security barriers and into the heart of Space Command Headquarters. There seemed to be thousands of scientists and engineers. Some were working at desks, some gathered in meetings, some fiddling with holographic design programs. Everyone looked busy and important. Sophie noticed the occasional second glance as if to say, "what are you children doing here?" Others smiled at them.

They followed Dr Millson to a meeting room full of smartly dressed people sat around a large table. The floor-to-ceiling window along the back of the room revealed a spectacular view of the rest of the spaceport. Sophie wondered if she could see her village in the distance. Dr Millson invited the children to take a seat.

Each adult introduced themselves with their name, job title and what they do at Space Command. Sophie kept repeating the first names in her head, just in case she needed them later. Working in the homeless centre had taught her that people like having their name remembered.

"I am delighted that we have selected the finest team of young people for this very special mission," announced Dr Millson. "Now, let me tell you what we have planned for you. As you know, people have been travelling to space for many decades now. Space travel has never been safer. There are hundreds of astronauts visiting distant planets as we speak."

"Really? Hundreds?" asked Sahil.

Dr Millson wasn't expecting to be interrupted or questioned on her facts.

"Yes, Sahil. Well, I think it's more than one hundred, anyway." Dr Millson glanced at one of her colleagues, who informed her that there were currently 94 astronauts in 'live operations'.

"Well, anyway," continued Dr Millson, "we are concerned that soon children are going to be born in space. We know nothing about how they will cope. No child has ever been. Therefore, we decided to launch a space mission that selected the most capable young people and send them to an unexplored world, far enough so that we could observe behaviour over an extended period. We expect your mission to take three months."

The four kids were concentrating hard on every word. Leena fiddled with her blonde hair. Sahil's knee jiggled up and down uncontrollably.

"You will be travelling on one of our newest star ships, Flourish, to another star system. This will involve a hyperdrive jump to the star system. You will then travel to a planet within that star system, monitor from above, and, if possible, land on the surface to collect samples. You will then return home to report your findings."

Goosebumps emerged on Sophie's arms once more. This was not just a short trip to one of the other seven planets in the solar system, which would be exciting enough; this was a trip to a distant star! She glanced at her teammates. Jack was grinning from ear to ear. Sahil's eyes had grown even wider than usual. Leena's mouth hung open.

"Which star system?" asked Sophie.

"Well, that is something we are still discussing," admitted Dr Millson. "We have three candidates, and we are comparing data on each. Eve, show the children the candidates."

Dr Millson's assistant, Eve, tapped some buttons on her tablet and holograms of three colourful, rotating planets floated above the table. A grey planet was labelled TOI 700d, a red planet labelled Kepler 186f, and a purple and blue planet labelled K2 18b. A wondrous gaze filled the faces of Jack and Sahil. Leena's expression revealed little.

Dr Millson approached one of the planets. "So, this grey, rocky planet is TOI 700d. We think it has a nitrogen-rich atmosphere. The length of a day is 34 Earth hours...."

Sophie's attention drifted from Dr Millson's voice, and she stared at the purple-tinged world. An image of her recurring dream flashed into her mind, with rocks raining down onto the trees. Purple trees.

"K2 18b!" interrupted Sophie. The suddenness and volume of her voice surprised the whole room, especially Dr Millson, who turned to look at Sophie with a startled expression.

"Excuse me, Sophie?"

"K2 18b. We need to go there."

Sahil let out an awkward giggle.

"What makes you say that, Sophie?" asked Dr Millson, looking over the top of her glasses.

Sophie immediately felt self-conscious and embarrassed. The truth was she thought it vaguely resembled the colour of the landscape in her recurring dreams, but she was not prepared to share this. The whole of Space Command and her new teammates would probably think she was crazy. Her head dropped towards her lap. "Sorry, it's just a feeling. Like a gut instinct. I don't know what it's based on." She then remembered her dream again and lifted her head to return Dr Millson's gaze. "But I really think we should go there."

Dr Millson stared at Sophie intensely. Her eyes then flicked to a couple of her colleagues before she eventually spoke somewhat nervously. "Ok, thank you, Sophie. We value opinions from all of you. But we will decide which star system you go to after considering a range of factors."

Dr Millson signalled to Eve to turn off the planet projections. There was an awkward silence before Space Command employees started to murmur to each other.

It's too late, thought Sophie. *They think I'm crazy.*

Eventually, Dr Millson changed the subject. "You won't be alone on your adventure. We have two special companions to help you. The first is Codey. Send Codey in, please."

The doors to the side of the room slid open, and a glistening white robot strolled in, motors whirring with each step. Codey stood upright and was around the same height as Leena, who was slightly shorter than the other three. His camera eyes focussed on the children and his mouth lit up as he spoke.

"Good morning. My name is Codey. I am the latest space exploration assistant robot. I look forward to travelling with you."

"This gets better and better!" exclaimed Jack. "Codey, dude, I can't wait to get to know you better!"

"Nice to meet you, Jack. I will be happy to help you with engineering duties," responded Codey in a computerised British accent.

"Codey has many tools integrated into his small body," Dr Millson said, "and he doesn't need to breathe air, so he might be able to go places that you can't. Codey, show the children a quick demonstration of your capabilities."

"With pleasure," said Codey. "Firstly, I can make my arms and legs longer to reach things."

Codey's legs extended until his head was almost touching the ceiling. His arms then stretched out to either side, above the heads of the Space Command employees.

"Wooah!" shouted Jack.

"For increased speed over flat surfaces, I have wheels built into my legs and feet."

Codey returned to his original height, and two wheels moved forwards from just under his knee joints and two much smaller ones on the front of his feet. He knelt, and the wheels propelled him around the table, leaning from side to side to steer around the people.

"That is so clever," said Sophie. Sahil started clapping.

Codey returned to the front of the table and stood up. "I can adapt my hands into different tool configurations. Firstly, a screwdriver." One of his fingers retracted into his body and was replaced by the screwdriver. He raised it into the air and then rotated it at high speed. "This is a spanner..."

"Thank you, Codey, that's enough for now," said Dr Millson. "I'm sure the children will be equally delighted to meet their other helper. Please let Biggles in."

The door slid open again, and a cream-coloured Golden Retriever bounded into the room, tail flicking back and forth.

"We have learnt that dogs are fantastic at making humans feel more relaxed on long space missions," said Dr Millson, "and Biggles is one of our favourite dogs at Space Command."

Biggles ran straight to Sophie and licked her hand. Sophie, who was still recovering from the stress of her earlier outburst, instantly started to feel better as she massaged the scruff of his neck. *Did Biggles know I needed a doggy hug?*

With the help of holographic images, Dr Millson and her colleagues continued to tell the children more about their mission, the ship and the rest of the training they would need to do. Sophie had never concentrated harder but was continuously distracted by the butterflies still fluttering away in her stomach. This was starting to feel very real. She looked around the table at the important looking adults and then out the window at the enormous rocket ships.

I am going to lead these three children to a distant star system.

Her hands were starting to shake, so she held them under the table, out of sight.

"The launch date is just six weeks away. You will be sleeping at Space Command during the week and returning home at weekends. You all brought your overnight bags, I hope?"

The children all nodded.

"We have a lot to go through. Let's get started."

Chapter Seven
Training

"The first task is to introduce you to your mentor," announced Dr Millson. "You will go for a one-to-one meeting to complete some administrative tasks and to provide the opportunity to ask as many questions as you like. Sophie, I will be your mentor, so please follow me."

Sophie said goodbye to the others. She felt slightly irritated at how confident both Jack and Sahil looked. They were bouncing with excitement, like children that had eaten too much sugar. Leena, on the other hand, was keeping her emotions to herself.

Sophie followed Dr Millson through a series of corridors and into a small room. The plaque on the door was engraved with "Dr Emily Millson", followed by a long string of letters showing her qualifications. Inside there was a desk with a holographic display, a small meeting table, a variety of pot plants, a water cooler and a sofa. Framed certificates covered one wall. Dr Millson invited Sophie to join her on the sofa.

"So, Sophie, how are you feeling?"

Sophie thought for a moment. Her tummy was turning inside out with nervous energy, and she was concerned about accidentally vomiting all over Dr Millson's fabric sofa.

She breathed deeply before speaking. "Can I be honest? A little overwhelmed."

"Let me get you a glass of water." Dr Millson stood up, wandered over to the cooler and started filling a glass. She continued speaking with her back to Sophie. "Do you have any questions for me before we start?"

Sophie let out an anxious laugh. "Hundreds."

Dr Millson handed Sophie the ice-cold water. "Well, which one do you want to start with?"

The glass trembled in Sophie's hand, which she tried to ignore as she looked Dr Millson straight in the eye. "Why me?"

Dr Millson looked surprised. "Why not you, Sophie?"

Sophie's eyes dropped to her lap. "I was just not expecting to be chosen. There were so many good candidates. Plus, I failed the first exercise."

"Sophie, look at me. Are you having second thoughts?"

"No, I've never wanted anything so much in my life, but...the ships are just so big, and there are so many people here, and I think about leading the other kids to another star system. I suppose I'm feeling a little," Sophie didn't want to say what immediately came to mind but failed to think of an alternative word quickly enough, "scared."

Dr Millson smiled. She looked thoughtfully at Sophie for a moment before speaking. "Let me own up to something. We were a little bit naughty. The first group exercise was impossible to pass. It was designed to see how candidates respond to disappointment. In space, things can and probably will go wrong, and there will be tough decisions to make. Your group was the only one that didn't destroy the ship and kill yourselves, and it was all because of you, Sophie. You took the necessary decisions. You managed your teammates effectively. You realised you didn't have a pilot, so you even bravely attempted to fly the ship based purely on your own research and without any formal training. You decided it was more important to save the lives of your teammates rather than follow the mission objective." Dr Millson took a sip of her water. "I don't think you are the type to get big-headed, so I don't mind telling you this. After just that first exercise, you convinced us you would be our captain. By the end of the selection process, you were light years ahead of all the other candidates, Sophie."

Sophie felt pride flooding into her body, and the nausea and self-doubt were disappearing. She could have cried, but she managed to hold herself together. She didn't know what to say other than "Thank you."

"Can I ask you a question now, Sophie?"

"Of course."

"Why planet K2 18b? During the briefing, you were insisting you go to that planet. Why?"

Sophie still didn't want to reveal the specifics of her dream, so she decided to keep it vague. "I can't explain it. It just feels like the planet is calling me. I feel like I need to, er, *we* need to go there."

Dr Millson raised her eyebrows.

"It's probably nothing," said Sophie, partly to fill the gap in conversation and partly to avoid Dr Millson losing confidence in her.

"Ok, well, K2 18b does look interesting, so we will continue to look at the data. Now we need to fill in some forms and get permission from your mother. Is it ok with you if we set up a call with her?"

Sophie nodded.

Dr Millson tapped a button on her watch and then spoke into it. "Eve, please set up a call with Mari Williams, and ask Stewart and Carmen to join us."

"Stewart is from our Human Resources department, and Carmen is one of our 'wellbeing' experts. We need them on the call to ensure I'm not pressuring you and your family into any decisions," said Dr Millson, almost apologetically.

A few minutes later, there was a knock on the door and in came Stewart and Carmen, both of whom were in their mid-twenties. They greeted Sophie enthusiastically and told her how much they had been looking forward to meeting her. Stewart had blond hair combed into a neat side parting and a Welsh accent, whilst Carmen had olive skin, dark hair and an accent that suggested she was originally from Spain or South America.

Everyone sat at the office table, and Mari appeared on the holographic display. "Hello Sophie, my love! Are they looking after you there? I tell you, it took me forever to get home in the traffic this morning. I've never seen anything like it. So, I was just talking to a nice lady, er, oh, I've forgotten her name now, what was her name?"

"Eve," both Sophie and Dr Millson said together.

"Yes, she said you wanted to talk to me. I've been waiting all day to find out what you're up to."

Eventually, Dr Millson got a chance to speak. "Good afternoon Mrs Williams. My name is Emily Millson. I am responsible for designing the mission, and I will also be Sophie's mentor through the training process. These are my colleagues, Stewart Henderson and Carmen Pérez. I'm here to explain what we have planned for your daughter. Please ask as many questions as you like. At the end of the meeting, I will be asking if you consent to Sophie's involvement in the mission."

"Ah, your name was on all those messages."

The meeting dragged on for more than two hours, partly because Mari loves to chat and partly because she kept asking questions, mainly along the lines of 'what happens if things go wrong'. Although many of the questions were embarrassing and highlighted Mari's lack of scientific knowledge, some were challenging even for Dr Millson to answer. Despite all of the procedures in place, Dr Millson eventually had to admit that the mission was not without risk. After all, it is space travel.

Sophie mostly stayed quiet throughout the call but occasionally interjected with comments like 'Mum, these people are very busy!'

Dr Millson, looking tired but still forcing a smile, eventually attempted to conclude the call. "So, Mrs Williams, do you have any more questions?"

To Sophie's relief, Mari responded with, "No, I think you've covered everything. I'll let you know if I think of anything else."

"Yes, please do. I now have to ask you a very important question. Do you consent to your daughter taking part in this mission?"

Sophie held her breath for what seemed like minutes before Mari let out a sigh and responded. "Yes, I do. Just make sure you have her home in one piece."

Over the coming weeks, Sophie thought her brain would explode with information. They were taught about every detail of the ship, the mission, and the indications regarding the star system they would be visiting. There were endless 'scenarios' to learn what to do should they encounter particular circumstances.

Then there was the physical training, which included being spun around on the astronaut training equivalent of a giant fairground ride. "The centrifuge will prepare your body for the huge G-forces you will experience on launch," said Dr Millson. Sophie was always okay with the spinny-roundy fairground rides, as she used to call them, so she enjoyed the thrill of her body being thrust to the back of her seat but was less keen on the sensation of her facial skin trying to move around to the back of her head. Leena and Sahil didn't seem to have any problems. Sahil got out of the centrifuge pod with his typical wide eyes and a broad grin, whilst Leena looked no different coming out as when she went in and just described it as "fine".

In contrast, Jack's usually dark skin had turned pale. He staggered out of the pod, leant forwards and took deep breaths with his hands on his thighs before sprinting towards the bathrooms. When he eventually emerged, he tried to put on a brave face and said he was fine but was unusually quiet for the rest of the afternoon.

One of the more enjoyable sessions was the spacewalk training. The kids were shown what was introduced to them as the world's largest swimming pool. It was located in a vast hanger with bright white walls and cranes on rails across the ceiling. The pool was filled with deep blue water and an array of replica rocket ships.

"Being underwater is a bit like zero-gravity," said Sahil before it started. "The only difference is the water-resistance. In space, it will be much easier to move around."

Space Command engineers showed the kids how to put their spacesuits on. Each suit had been tailored to each child's body, based on a full-body scan, but the material was slightly stretchy to allow room for the child to grow. Sophie wriggled her body into it. Once she had pushed her fingers to the end of the gloves, and her feet slotted into the boots, which looked more like running shoes with their light and modern design, it fitted perfectly. She then snapped the mask over her face, and oxygen began to flow into her lungs. The air felt pure and clean.

Catching sight of herself in a reflective window, the realisation kicked in. It was no longer a twelve-year-old schoolgirl looking back at her. It was an astronaut. She really was going to space. The adventure was becoming scarily real.

"The suit is completely voice-activated," said Chuck, a stocky man with an impressive moustache. Originally from Texas, Chuck had a strong, southern-USA accent. "Just say hi to your suit, and it will fire up."

"Hello spacesuit," said Sophie, a little nervously.

"Good morning, Sophie," replied a comforting female voice in an American accent. Writing appeared on the helmet visor in front of her. It showed the oxygen level in the tanks and many other readings such as temperature, pressure, current location and velocity.

"Ok, kids. Jump in when you're ready."

Sophie couldn't resist the instinct of holding her breath as she plunged into the swimming pool, but there was no need as the suit was providing all of her air, as it would if she was in space.

A replica part of their spaceship was suspended underwater. The kids had to work as a team to fix a broken panel. Jack was in his element. He talked to the group over the radios, which were built into the suits. "Sophie, I know you normally like to tell me what to do, but fixing stuff is kinda my thing, so do you mind if I take charge?"

"Be my guest, Jack," replied Sophie.

Between them, they had figured out which tools to use and had the panel replaced in no time.

"Well, we didn't expect you to finish this exercise quite so quickly," announced Chuck over the radio. "But as we have time to spare, I may as well show you something else. Now, let me just be clear, the chances that you will need to spacewalk as part of this mission are minimal. If you do need to, you will be tethered to the ship. There is virtually no chance that the tether can break – do you hear me?"

"Yes, sir," responded Sahil.

"But, if the tether were to break, you have a backup rocket pack in the spacesuit. I might as well explain how it works."

Chuck told them how to access two small joysticks from the sleeves of the suit, one for each hand. The joysticks controlled jets, which expelled gas from the rear, propelling the children forward. Jack was the first to try them and pushed the joysticks forwards far too quickly. He fired himself straight into the side of the rocket.

"Hey, those suits are expensive!" shouted Chuck.

Leena eased one of her joysticks forwards and the other slightly to the side. Within seconds she was circling her teammates, performing twists and spirals.

"Leena, no one likes a show-off," said Jack, who was still stuttering forwards and back.

"Ha! Look who's talking!" said Sophie.

"What? I'm not a show-off."

"Jack, I still remember the first virtual exercise we did together when you introduced yourself as the master engineer."

Sahil and Leena laughed over their radios. Jack ignored them. He was still too busy trying to master his jet pack.

Dr Millson was waiting for Sophie as she changed out of her spacesuit. "Sophie, we've made a decision about the planet you will be visiting. I thought you would like to know."

"Yes, please!"

"We compared all of the data, and the most promising planet was actually Kepler 186f..."

Oh, no! They are not sending us to K2 18b, thought Sophie. She suddenly felt like she was letting someone down. The creature from her dreams lived on a purple planet, and desperately needed help.

"...but, the decision was a marginal one. TOI 700d also looks very promising..."

Something terrible will happen. If we don't go to K2 18b, something terrible is going to happen.

"...but, to be honest, there wasn't much to choose between them. In the end, I decided we should follow your instinct, Sophie. You will be going to planet K2 18b."

Oh, thank goodness!

Sophie threw her arms around Dr Millson, who clearly wasn't expecting the embrace as she staggered backwards.

"Thank you, Dr Millson. I'm sure you won't regret it."

Dr Millson released a nervous laugh. "Hopefully, you're right Sophie."

Chapter Eight
Restaurant

On weekday evenings, the children were staying in the on-site hotel. They each had their own room, which Dr Millson told them was kitted out a little as their rooms would be on the spaceship. *Early training for the mission,* thought Sophie. *See how we cope in hotel rooms for a few weeks before sending us for months in the space equivalent.*

They decided to have dinner together in the hotel restaurant every evening. The restaurant had an aquatic theme, with ropes and pictures of old sailing ships on the walls. A large anchor, which must have belonged to a huge ship, sat on a plinth in the centre. Sahil suggested the theme was recognising explorers of the past, whose ships floated on the ocean rather than in space.

On this particular evening, Leena and Sophie arrived at the restaurant before the boys and sat at their usual table next to an impressive fish tank. Leena was staring at the two most spectacular fish in the tank, which, after some debate, was agreed to be a pair of Threadfin Butterflyfish. They were large and flat, with yellow tails and chevron markings across their vibrant blue bodies.

"Leena, I was amazed how quickly you got the hang of controlling your spacesuit. You were whizzing around like a dolphin!" said Sophie.

"Yeah, thanks. It was pretty easy, I thought."

There were a few seconds of awkward silence. "So, how do you feel about everything, Leena?"

"It's fine. Good."

It bothered Sophie that she and Leena had never really talked much, and she found the response from Leena frustrating. From Sophie's perspective, this whole experience was much more than just 'fine' and 'good'. It was the most life-changing, overwhelming, terrifying and exhilarating thing she had ever done. She decided to challenge Leena.

"Come on, how are you really feeling? You know we are going to be in space together for months. We must be able to communicate and let each other know what's on our minds."

Leena suddenly looked concerned. "Sorry, Sophie. I, er..." There was a long pause. "I'm fine, but I'm not very good at...The thing is, I'm..."

Leena shuffled in her seat whilst Sophie waited patiently for the answer, listening intently. Just as Leena was about to speak again, Sahil arrived.

"Good evening, ladies. It's very nice to make your acquaintance on this fine evening."

Sahil's over-the-top greeting amused Sophie, but the timing could not have been worse. She really wanted to hear what Leena was going to say. Then a moment later, Jack arrived. "Hey Leena, Sahil, boss-girl!"

Their normal waiter, Tom, came over to their table. Tom was 18, so only six years older than the kids, and felt more like one of them than an adult. He had a ridiculous amount of bushy ginger hair and a fun personality to match.

Tom placed a jug of water in the middle of the table with four glasses. "Ok, you lot. Let me guess," he began in his joyful Welsh accent, "Jack, you want the club sandwich with fries and no salad, even though we have to give you salad because the bosses told us to make sure you eat healthily, and salad is an integral part of a club sandwich!"

"You got it, Thomas, my man! But at least no tomayto. I hate when the tomayto sauce contaminates the good stuff."

"Jack, we're in Britain. It's to-***mar***-to. You have to learn our language! Ok, I'll ask the chef to swap your to-**may**-to for a side of broccoli. Leena, seafood salad? Sahil, curry with rice, and you're going to tell me we shouldn't call it curry because of some reason I can't remember, and it's nowhere near as good as what your granny makes, but we'll add some extra spice to help it go down for you, and Sophie, the veggie lasagne?"

The kids nodded and laughed, except Leena, who was looking increasingly uncomfortable. When Tom headed to the kitchen, Leena kept glancing from side to side, opening her mouth as if about to talk and then not talking.

Sophie started pouring a glass of water for each of them. She passed one to Leena. "Leena, are you ok?"

"I'm autistic," came the sudden response. Jack and Sahil's eyes widened. They both froze in surprise.

"I want to tell all of you because I think you need to know. I'm autistic, and I'm not good with emotions. Sophie, you asked me how I'm feeling, and I feel lots of things, but I'm bad at talking about them. I'm good at concentrating on things, which is probably why I'm good at flying spaceships, but I'm not good at, er, conversation and stuff. I also think very literally, so complicated sentences, especially in English, I find them very confusing." Leena's face was turning red as if what she was saying was making her angry. "Sahil, you said hello when you arrived and something about making an acquaintance? I had no idea what you were talking about. What even is that?"

Her head dropped, and she stared at the table. "Sorry."

Sophie felt terrible and was desperately thinking of something to say. Thankfully, Sahil broke the silence. "Leena, thank you for sharing this. I can assure you; you are not the only one who finds what I say confusing."

"Hey, I thought I was the only one who didn't understand anyone!" said Jack, laughing. "Especially Sophie with her Welsh accent and weird expressions."

Sophie ignored Jack and turned to Leena. "Leena, I'm sorry I pushed you earlier. Thank you for telling us. Many of the greatest people in history had autism, and you will probably be considered one of them. Your piloting skills are truly amazing."

Leena continued looking at the table as she spoke. "My parents were both pilots. My dad flew space tourists to Mars, and my mum worked for a space mining company. When I was born, they gave it all up and bought a farm in Finland, which they managed mainly with drones. They let me start flying them from the age of two, and they just made sense to me. I've always found machines so much easier to understand than people."

"That is why Space Command selected you for this," said Jack. "Honestly, I've never seen anyone master the control system of a jet-propelled space suit so quickly."

"That's not much of a compliment, Jack," said Sahil. "Have you ever seen anyone using a jet-propelled space suit before today?"

"Look, the point is," interrupted Sophie, "we need to get to know each other if this mission is going to be a success. We need to understand each other. We need to be honest with each other. That's why I'm so happy that you were able to tell us what you did, Leena."

Leena looked up and smiled. Her eyes then flicked up to something above Jack's head. A tiny spider was descending from the ceiling on a strand of silk.

"Looks like you've got a new friend, Jack," said Sophie.

"What?" Jack looked directly upwards just as the spider dropped straight onto his face.

Jack exploded in panic. "Arrggghh! Get it off." He jumped up from his chair and knocked his glass of water, which streamed across the table and all over Sophie's jeans. The glass rolled off the table and smashed on the tiled floor. He then continued to wave his arms, trying to rid himself of the tiny creature.

Leena stood up. "Keep still!" she shouted. Jack froze, other than his trembling hands. The spider was motionless on the side of his head. Leena calmly finished her glass of water and picked up the paper menu. She placed the glass over the spider and then slid the menu between Jack's head and the glass, trapping the spider. Leena strolled outside and released Jack's new friend into the bushes. She returned and sat back down as if nothing had happened.

"Well, I think we now know a bit more about you now, Jack!" said Sophie whilst attempting to dry her jeans with napkins.

"I'm sorry, Sophie," Jack said between heavy breaths. "Thanks, Leena. Yeah, I don't know why, but maybe you should know that I hate spiders. Oh no! Here comes Tom. He's going to find this hilarious."

Chapter Nine
Blast Off

Wednesday, 10th April 2069, 9:42 am

It felt like no time at all before Sophie found herself strapped into her seat on the control deck of the giant star ship, preparing to lead her team of three other children, a robot and a dog to a distant star system.

Leena's pilot chair was at the front of the cabin, and she had an array of touchscreen displays, joysticks and controls within easy reach. Jack was on the right with his engineering panel, and Sahil was to the left at the scientific monitoring station. Biggles was strapped into a special seat known to the engineers as the canine zero-gravity restraining platform, although Sophie just called it the doggy chair. He looked the most confident out of all of them. Codey was docked into his charging point behind Jack.

Sophie was in her captain's chair, which was further back, enabling her to see everyone. The layout looked very similar to their training programmes in the simulators, although simulators couldn't recreate everything. The smell reminded Sophie of the first time she got into her dad's new car when she was young.

The ship was parked on the launchpad, which meant the chairs were facing directly upwards, and the children were more lying on their back rather than sitting. The front wall was covered in monitors displaying views in all directions, with the largest screen focussed directly ahead towards the sky. It was a beautiful, sunny day. Just one or two fluffy clouds separated the children from the vast expanse of space.

Space Command designers clearly favoured cream as their colour of choice for all of the moulded plastic units. Every last cubic centimetre of space had been designed to be functional but also neat and tidy. Sophie loved it. She closed her eyes for a few seconds and tried to comprehend what she was about to do. In just a few minutes, she was going to space. That sick feeling started to return to her stomach, as it had for most of the morning, from first waking up, to going through the final training with Dr Millson and the rest of the engineers, to boarding the ship.

The voices of Space Command engineers were coming through fast on the ship's radio.

"Flourish launch sequence initiation. Full system check. LTT?"

"LTT – go."

"FPP?"

"FPP – go."

"Safety combo?"

"Safety combo - go."

"APN?"

"APN – go."

The questions continued for several minutes. Sophie now knew what all the letters stood for, although she still hated that engineers seemed to speak more in letters than words.

"Flourish, this is Space Command. Please report your ship's status."

Finally, this was Sophie's turn. She swallowed back a little bit of sick that had forced its way up from her stomach and tried her best to sound calm and professional. She had practised this many times.

"Jack, engineering systems status?"

Jack checked his screen. "Engineering systems – go, Captain."

"Leena, launch systems status?"

"Launch systems – go, Captain."

Sophie took one last deep breath. This was it. "Space Command, this is Flourish. We're ready for launch, over."

"Flourish, you are clear for launch. Initiate launch sequence."

"Last chance to stay on Earth!" said Jack.

"You must be joking!" responded Sahil.

"Leena, take us up," instructed Sophie.

Leena tapped a series of buttons. "Initiating launch."

A computerised female voice started the countdown. "Flourish launch in 10, 9, 8, 7, 6...

Rocket packs thundered into life, a noise Sophie could feel as much as she could hear. Plumes of fire and smoke erupted, and the new car smell was replaced by that of rocket fuel.

"....5, 4, 3, 2, 1, lift-off."

The giant, circular spaceship shook and rattled. Rockets pushed the enormous weight of the ship off the ground, slowly at first and then rapidly accelerating upwards, forcing the children down into their seats. Leena concentrated hard on her controls. Sophie's internal organs were pressing into her spine.

Sahil's eyes were like saucepan lids. "We're doing it. We are actually doing it!" he screamed. He had the look of a young kid who had just unwrapped the toy of his dreams and the widest grin Sophie had ever seen.

The spaceport was soon just a dot on the spaceship monitors. The outline of countries and continents became visible, as did the long curve of the Earth. Half the planet was in brilliant sunshine, and half was in darkness with blobs of artificial light shining from the large cities. Ahead of them, the blue sky had darkened, revealing a blanket of stars. Of all the fantastic views across the various monitors, it was the majestic sight of the Earth from space that mesmerised Sophie the most.

The roar continued for several minutes. "We are beyond Earth's gravity," said Leena, tapping buttons. "Disengaging rockets." The rockets fell silent as her ponytail drifted above her head.

Sophie pressed a button to open the radio channel. "Space Command, this is Flourish. We have completed the rocket burn. Launch successful, over."

The kids heard a cheer and applause before the official response came back from a Space Command engineer. "Roger that, Flourish. Congratulations on making history. A lot of people down here are very excited about what you're doing. You are clear to start preparations for the hyperjump, over."

Sophie switched off the radio, and the four children looked at each other in disbelief. "Well, it's official. We are now the first-ever kids to go to space!" announced Sophie.

"Oh yeah, baby!" shouted Jack, followed by what looked like a spasm of air punching.

"What are we waiting for?" asked Sahil, still with a childish grin. "Let's try out some zero-gravity!" He then looked at Sophie. "Sorry, Captain, can we try zero-gravity?"

Sophie smiled, "Yes, of course."

The kids unbuckled. There was nothing to pull them to the floor. The slightest push on her chair propelled Sophie up from her seat. She glided effortlessly forwards until she hit Leena, who was coming the other way. The two girls burst out laughing.

Jack had accidentally got into a spin and couldn't stop himself. "Arrggghhhh! I feel like I'm gonna chuck! Someone stop me."

Sophie pushed herself off Leena, nudging her into a screen, and grabbed Jack's leg to slow him down.

Sahil was hanging upside down, still with a huge grin. "Whatever you do, do not vomit without a sick bag," he advised. "Remember what they said about how undesirable it is to have the regurgitated contents of your stomach floating around in the control deck." He then pushed off a panel to launch himself over to Biggles and unbuckled him from his special dog seat. Biggles barked with excitement as he tried to doggy paddle from one person to another, with drops of saliva escaping from his tongue and floating into the air.

"Oh – I need to record this!" exclaimed Sophie. She nudged herself over to a cupboard and pulled out a small camera. "Dr Millson told us to record videos to send back to Earth."

Jack was starting to get the hang of zero-gravity and regain his composure. "I need a drink," he announced as he grabbed a water bottle from a compartment and then noticed Sophie had started recording.

"Oh, wait, I've always wanted to try this." Jack took the bottle and squirted out a small amount of water. The perfect sphere of liquid floated like a ping pong ball on a string. He opened his mouth wide, intending to swallow it, but to his horror, he miscalculated the speed, and the shimmering ball collided with his face. Because there was no gravity, it remained stuck to his right eye.

"Ahhh! Get it off!" Jack shouted.

"Jack, you're an idiot!" said Leena before calmly pushing herself over to another compartment, grabbing a towel and gliding towards him. "Keep still," she said as she dabbed his eye dry.

Sophie rolled her eyes and tried not to laugh. "Let's show everyone the ship. Leena, please activate the artificial gravity."

"Yes, captain." Leena pushed herself back to her controls and tapped a few buttons. "Starting ship rotation."

The outside of the ship started to spin like a bicycle wheel. The control deck was in the centre and was like the wheel's hub, always at zero-gravity. The living areas, kitchen, bedrooms, and almost everything else was in the outer part. What connected the two was a narrow corridor which contained a ladder. This ladder was a strange experience because, at the top of it, there was no gravity. At the bottom, it was the same as on Earth.

"Remember to go down feet first," Sahil reminded the others. "If you go head first, you will finish upside down at the bottom and getting off will be, er, tricky."

The four of them descended the ladder and felt gravity gradually increasing with each rung. Codey followed the children and looked far more graceful, probably because he was pre-programmed on ladder use.

Sophie looked back up to the top of the ladder. Biggles was still scrambling around in the control deck with his ears floating uncontrollably, which made him look a bit like a bat. He was trying to doggy paddle towards the ladder.

Sophie encouraged him. "Come on, Biggles. Here boy!"

Biggles eventually caught the first rung with his paw and took the first few slowly before increasing speed, losing control and ending up in a heap on the floor.

Leena gave him a stroke. "Don't worry, Biggles. You'll get better at it."

Sophie pointed her camera at Jack. "Jack, please explain to everyone what we have on board."

"Ok, captain," Jack replied.

"Look, guys, don't call me captain! It sounds weird!"

"Ok, boss," said Jack with a grin.

"Jack, just call me Soph!" snapped Sophie, forgetting the camera was running, which would broadcast her outburst to everyone on Earth. She remembered her mum saying she was a 'right little bossy boots', and being referred to as 'boss' by Jack was always irritating. She then realised raising her voice at Jack was another example of bossiness.

Fortunately, Jack didn't notice and started speaking to the camera as if he was on a TV commercial. "Hey, everyone! I'm Jack, the master-engineer and now one of the first-ever children to go into space." He paused to wink at the camera. "So, these big corridors have lots of storage built-in, but they are good for exercising. We can run around in normal gravity. Biggles can exercise here as well when he's not falling down ladders. Watch this."

Jack pulled out a rubber ball from his pocket before raising his voice several octaves to talk to the dog. "Biggles! What's this boy?" Biggles trotted over with his bright eyes fixed on the ball. Jack launched it along the corridor, and Biggles sprinted after it, claws clattering against the spaceship floor, and caught it on the fourth bounce. He skidded, raced back, dropped the ball at Jack's feet and stared up at him, tail wagging.

"Codey, please carry on throwing the ball for Biggles," said Jack.

"No problem." Codey picked up the ball and threw it. "Biggles, fetch!" he said in his robotic voice. The kids laughed. They had never seen a robot playing ball with a dog before.

Jack continued along the corridor. "Ok, this room is our virtual playroom. Think of it as a big computer game that feels very real, as if you are actually there."

"This is not just to stop us from getting bored," interrupted Sahil to the camera, "it's been proven that if you are stuck on a spaceship for many months, it's good to pretend to be somewhere else for a while."

Sophie turned the camera to Leena, who ducked to avoid being on video. "Don't be shy, Leena. Tell everyone about the games."

"Ok, er, we have lots of games we can play, either on our own or together," she said whilst trying to fix her hair which was still recovering from zero-gravity. "I like the racing driver game."

"That's only because you always win!" complained Jack.

"You beat me once, Jack. Remember the time I got rammed off the course by the computer driver?"

"Yeah, once out of 300 games!"

Sophie tried to bring the conversation back to the tour of the spaceship. "Jack, why don't you show people the hyperdrive?"

"Ok, folks, this is the exciting bit." Jack entered a circular room. In the centre was a metal frame supporting a glowing green ball of plasma. "This is the cutting-edge technology that lets us travel to the stars. Welcome—" he paused for dramatic effect, "—to the hyperdrive! Sahil, you can explain how it works better than I can."

"So, the trouble with space," said Sahil, "is that it is very, very, very, very big. In fact, you cannot really imagine how big it actually is. To get to stars using normal rockets would take many thousands of years. Even if we were travelling as fast as light, which we can't with rockets, but if we could, it would take four years to get to our nearest star. To the centre of our galaxy of stars would take 26,000 years, and to other galaxies, it would take—"

"Yes, we get the idea," interrupted Sophie, "so tell people what the hyperdrive does."

"Well, imagine if you have a long piece of paper. At one end, you draw a spaceship, and at the other, you draw the star you're trying to reach. Normally to get between the two, you need to travel along a straight line on the piece of paper. But then imagine if you can pick up the piece of paper and bend it over, so the spaceship and the star are in the same place. The hyperdrive does this and then punches through to create a hole that we can travel through. We call this a wormhole. It bends space and creates a shortcut to make the distance between two points much smaller."

"That is so cool," said Sophie, staring past her camera and into the green glow. "I've not seen it switched on before. Leena, let's show them Spacebug."

"Oh, yeah," said Leena, growing in confidence. Leena jogged out of the hyperdrive room and down the corridor. She opened a door that was labelled cargo bay 3. Lights flicked on as she entered, revealing the metallic floor and walls. Pipework and ducting covered the ceiling. Two massive doors, painted in yellow and black diagonal stripes, covered the rear wall. These were doors to outer space.

A sleek little spaceship stood in the centre of the room, with polished chrome bodywork gleaming under the cargo bay strip lights.

"Spacebug is for flying down to the surface of planets," continued Leena. "We can't take the whole ship down because it's too heavy and we wouldn't have enough fuel to take off again, but Spacebug is like a small sports car, compared to Flourish, which is like a big bus."

"Ok, everyone," concluded Sophie turning the camera off, "it's time to talk directly to people on Earth before we set off for K2-18. Remember, once we travel with the hyperdrive, we won't be able to communicate with Earth because we will be too far away, and we may be some time, so enjoy these last moments. Meet back on the control deck in 30 minutes."

The four children headed to their bedrooms to talk privately with their families and friends. The Space Command psychologists decided the children should be involved in the design of their bedrooms and should make them feel as homely as possible. Sophie's colour scheme matched her bedroom on Earth, and she sat on her bed looking at her picture of dad.

Sophie had a list of people to call. The first was Dr Millson. She tapped the button, and Dr Millson popped up on her holographic display. Sophie was expecting to see her in the Space Command briefing room but was surprised to see her headteacher, Mrs Jenkins, and the school sports hall in the background. "Dr Millson, why are you at my school?"

"Hi, Sophie", she said in a cheerful voice, "firstly, congratulations on being one of the first children ever to go to space. Now I was talking to your headteacher, Mrs Jenkins," Dr Millson continued. "She wanted to give you a special message from the school."

The display turned to reveal over one thousand kids sat on plastic chairs looking directly at her. Mrs Jenkins came to the front and started to speak in her posh voice.

"Well, Sophie, this is exciting. This is the first time I've ever spoken to someone who's in space."

Mrs Jenkins took off her glasses. "Sophie, I think I speak for all of the teachers when I say you represent the very embodiment of what our school is all about. You have dedicated yourself to helping push the boundaries of human exploration. I know how much work you needed to put into your Space Command application. Not only this, but I found out recently you were giving up much of your free time to help at the homeless shelter, which is so thoughtful for the wellbeing of others. You have proved yourself to be an inspiration to everyone at this school and children around the world. You have certainly inspired Mr Galway – he talks about nothing else in the staff room!"

There was a murmur of laughter from across the hall. Mr Galway was laughing and nodding as if he didn't mind being the source of amusement given the circumstances.

Sophie was still trying to get her head around how many children were staring at her. Most of the kids were older and considerably bigger than her. *Don't cry. Please don't cry.* In the front row, Josh, Dylan and Adian were holding up a banner covered in stars, planets, rockets and the words 'Go Space Girl'. Josh waved, and Sophie waved back.

"Now I know you're very busy, Sophie," continued Mrs Jenkins, "but we wanted to give you a message. Okay, everybody, on the count of three. One, two, three!"

The whole school spoke in one overwhelmingly loud voice. "GOOD LUCK SOPHIE! WE ARE PROUD OF YOU!" Sophie's eyes started to fill with tears, ignoring her earlier instructions from her brain.

Sophie felt the urge to thank a couple of people individually. "Mr Galway, thank you for all your support."

Mr Galway raised his hand with a beaming grin.

"And thank you, Josh, for all of your help! I couldn't have done it without you."

The whole school turned to catch a glimpse of Josh, who giggled nervously. Aiden ruffled his hair affectionately.

"Thank you, everybody. You have no idea what this means to me!"

The camera swung back to Mrs Jenkins. "And good luck from me, Sophie. We can't wait to hear your stories when you get back."

The display then turned to Dr Millson. "Now just remember Sophie," she whispered, "space travel has never been safer, but it can never be absolutely safe, so be careful and don't take any unnecessary risks."

"I promise," replied Sophie, wiping away a tear. "Thank you for believing in me and trusting me to do this."

"You deserve this chance, Sophie. Enjoy every moment of it."

The display vanished. Sophie was alone in her bedroom once more. *Ok, what's next.* She glanced at her pictures. *Mum.* A couple of taps on the controls, and Mari popped up, sat in the kitchen with a mug of tea in front of her.

"Hi mum!" she said with a smile.

"Is that my space girl? Hi sweetheart," she replied. "Oh, Sophie, I've been waiting all day for this. I've been a bag of nerves. When I watched your rocket ship going up, I couldn't believe it was you in there. Do you know it was on the news, and they showed your picture? I felt so...wait a minute, have you been crying?"

"No, I'm fine, mum, well, yes, I cried a little bit, but it was happy crying. I'm fine!"

Her mum's expression turned more serious. "Now, you take care of yourself, Sophie Williams. Promise me that you will be careful wherever it is you're going!"

Sophie could see the worry in her mum's face. She suddenly felt bad. If something terrible happened on the mission, mum would be alone. This had not occurred to her before and caused a surge of guilt. Sophie knew mum was also still recovering from losing dad, even more than she was. Was it selfish to want to do this? Should she have stayed at home and supported her?

"What's the matter?" her mum asked, sensing her sudden change of mood.

"Will you be ok, mum?" Sophie asked.

"Sophie, it's so typical of you to worry about others. I'll be absolutely fine. Now you go and get that mission of yours done, and I'll have a nice apple pie waiting for you when you get home."

Chapter Ten
Jump

The children climbed back up the ladder and floated into the control deck of the ship. Jack whistled to Biggles, who came doggy paddling in, still grasping his ball in his mouth.

"Ok, boy," said Jack. "I'll look after your ball. Let's buckle you in, ready for the hyperdrive jump."

Leena's fingers danced over her controls. The ship turned to face the right direction.

Sophie had read many books about hyperdrive jumps and what had gone wrong with them over the years. She decided to seek some reassurance. "Sahil, remind us all what this will feel like."

"Oh! It's going to be a bumpy ride, I think," replied Sahil. "People say it is impossible to describe because it's not like anything experienced on Earth. Maybe something like extreme pins and needles. Our bodies will be bending the rules of physics."

"What does that mean?" asked Leena.

Codey responded. "Einstein's theory of special relativity states that space and time are...."

"It's ok, thanks, Codey," interrupted Sophie, "we can save the lesson for another day. Let's just do it. Leena, input coordinates for K2-18."

"Coordinates set," confirmed Leena. "Hold tight. On my countdown, three, two, one, launch!"

The Hyperdrive engine boomed into life and hummed as the ship started to rattle. A sudden, deafening clap of thunder startled the children and terrified Biggles, who buried his head into his seat. The ship jolted from side to side.

"That must be the wormhole opening! I think this is normal!" shouted Sahil at the top of his voice, attempting to reassure the team even though he couldn't stop his own hands from trembling. "There it is!"

A black sphere had formed in front of the ship, surrounded by a glow of blue light. Clusters of distant stars and swirling gases of nebulae were visible within the sphere. Lightning danced around it, and the air within the spaceship felt like it was crackling with static electricity. The wormhole was growing on the front display as the ship accelerated towards it.

"Take it steady, Leena," instructed Sophie. "Not too fast."

"I'm not touching the controls!" responded Leena.

Sahil was studying the readings on his display. "The gravity of the wormhole is pulling us in. There is no way we can avoid it now - we just have to relax and enjoy the ride."

Suddenly, the crackling gave way to a whoosh as the children were thrown back in their seats. The ship raced into the wormhole like a rollercoaster plummeting down a vertical track.

"My body feels all tingly!" screamed Jack. "This is so weird!"

"Hold on, everyone!" yelled Sophie.

The ship creaked and groaned. Blurs of bright light flashed at the windows. The tingling ran through every cell of Sophie's body. She lifted her hand, which seemed to split into five transparent hands, and she tried to shake it back into one, but it didn't work. Her hand shaking seemed to happen in slow motion, and she had no idea which was her actual hand. Maybe they all were.

Sophie glanced at her teammates. There were at least five versions of each of them, all in slightly different positions. Jack's left arm was simultaneously gripping the arm of his seat, touching his control panel and somewhere in between.

Everything was slowing more and more. One copy of Biggles started to let out a slow-motion bark which progressively slowed even more and lowered in pitch until it was more of a low growl than a bark.

And then, suddenly, everything returned to normal speed and merged back into one. All fell silent and still.

Leena looked at her screen whilst breathing heavily. "Er, I think we are now in star system K2-18."

The kids looked at each other and burst out laughing with a mix of shock and relief.

Sweat glistened from Sophie's forehead. "Well, that was more intense than I was expecting! Was anyone else seeing five of everything?"

"At least!" replied Jack. "Sahil, you were just a blur. I swear you had about ten twin brothers at one point. Then, time almost froze! I thought I was going to be stuck in the wormhole for ages. It was very weird."

"Yes, I saw it too. I have read about this phenomenon," replied Sahil. "Sometimes space and time go a little bit, er, out of phase, I think."

"Well, I'm very happy to be back in phase now!" said Sophie, wiping her forehead with her shirt sleeve. "Ok, let's have a look at this star system. Sahil, put the star up on the front screen."

"With pleasure Sophie." Sahil tapped at his control panel. "Ok, ladies and gentlemen, or boys, girls, robots and dogs, I should say, we will be the first humans ever to see Star K2-18 up close. Drum roll, please..."

Jack started drumming his engineering panel in anticipation whilst Sahil's finger hovered over the button.

"Sahil, just press it!" ordered Sophie.

"Sorry." Sahil tapped his screen again, and a fiery, red disc filled the front display.

Hairs on Sophie's arms stood up as she stared into it. "It's beautiful," she whispered.

"I will start collecting readings from the long-range sensors," said Sahil.

"Soph, we've got a problem," reported Leena. "Our hyperdrive jump took us off course. We are very far from planet K2-18b."

Sophie blinked. "How far?"

"At full speed, it will take more than a year to get to the planet," said Leena in a low voice.

The children's heads dropped as they realised what this would mean. They wouldn't be able to get to the planet without spending a whole year in space.

"A year? Soph, I didn't sign up for a year. I promised my best friend I'd be back for her birthday party in five months," said Jack.

Sophie initially thought this was another of Jack's bad jokes, but then a tear formed in his eye. He was serious. Sophie thought about her mum being alone for a whole year, which made her shiver. "Come on, guys, let's think about this. What options do we have?"

"Can we do another small hyperdrive jump?" asked Leena.

"No, we can't use it over small distances, and anyway, it takes months to recharge," responded Jack.

"Are there any other planets on route?" asked Sophie.

"But we're here to see K2-18b," said Jack. "The other planets look boring."

"I'm not planning on visiting them, just to use them for a fly-by."

Sahil knew what Sophie was thinking. "Ah – a slingshot? If we can pass close to another planet, we can use its gravity to speed us up."

"There is a huge gas planet, K2-18e, which is close to our route," said Leena, "but it's going too fast for us to catch it. We would need twice our maximum speed to get to it. But if we could, it would massively speed us up."

Suddenly, Jack's eyes lit up. He wiped away the tears. "Codey, how much fuel would it take to reach the speed needed?"

"It would take seven million litres to reach the required velocity to—"

"And how much do we have in total?" interrupted Jack.

"There are just over nine million litres in the fuel tanks."

"Soph, I have an idea," said Jack in a determined voice, "rockets work by pushing stuff out of the back, which pushes us forwards. I just need to adjust our rockets to push it out faster."

"Will that be safe, Jack?" replied Sophie.

"Of course. I will need to adjust a few things, but trust me - I've been building rockets since I was five years old. This one is just a bit bigger. The only problem is we will use up a lot of our fuel in this big push. If we don't get close enough to the gas planet, we will never get to see planet K2-18b."

"Jack, you give me the power, and I'll make sure we get close!" said Leena.

"Codey, how long will it take to reach K2-18b if we swing past the gas planet?" asked Sophie.

Codey's neck motor whirred as he turned to Sophie. "Depending on the exact path, 43 days."

Less than two months! Sophie was about to tell Jack to just get on with it, but then she remembered Dr Millson's advice. *Don't take unnecessary risks.*

How can I make sure Jack isn't doing anything risky? Sophie was confident in Jack's abilities. She had read all about his previous achievements. He wasn't just good with rockets; he was a genius with rockets. He won countless rocket-building contests, even beating many grown-ups that did it for their job. But this was far bigger than anything he had done before, and the consequences of an error would be catastrophic. There were enormous quantities of power and energy involved. The safest thing to do would be to just float in space for a few months and wait for the hyperdrive to recharge so they could go back home, but that didn't seem like much of a plan. Plus, deep down, she was becoming increasingly sure that something, or someone, from planet K2-18b was calling her.

Perhaps all Jack needs is someone to watch over him and reduce the chance of any mistake.

"Ok, Jack, you and Codey will go to work on the adjustments. However, I want you to explain everything to Sahil." Sophie turned to Sahil and looked directly into his eyes with intensity. "Sahil, you will oversee safety. You let me know if you have any doubts about the changes."

Sahil looked a little nervous. "Yes, Sophie, I will watch closely."

"Ok, Jack," said Sophie, "go and work your magic."

"Yes, boss!"

The boys and Codey headed down the ladder.

"Soph, I'm going to plan the route around the gas planet in more detail," suggested Leena.

"Good idea. I'm going to my room to write up what we've done so far."

Biggles was still strapped into his seat and looking at Sophie expectantly. "Come on, dog, come and help me!"

Biggles' ladder descending technique was improving with each attempt. Sophie led him into her bedroom and sat on her bed. She projected her logbook in front of her and started scribbling notes, but Biggles jumped onto the bed also and kept licking her hand.

"Biggles, out of the way!" said Sophie, laughing.

Biggles ignored her and kept pushing his nose into her hand.

"Look, I need to do this!"

Sophie gave Biggles a gentle shove off the bed. Biggles' head dropped, and he looked up at her with puppy dog eyes.

"Oh, come here then. I suppose this is all quite stressful for you as well, isn't it?"

Abandoning her work, Sophie patted the bed. Biggles wagged his tail and jumped onto it. His soft fur felt wonderful as she stroked it. Her eyelids started to feel heavy.

As Sophie drifted off to sleep, she once more found herself underwater. The yellow-eyed creature appeared clearer than even and was staring into her eyes.

"Who are you? Are you on K2-18b?"

"Sophie, you must arrive soon. Please."

"We're close. We're doing our best."

Sophie knew if she stayed in the dream, the vision of the rocks raining from the sky would return, and the thought of them filled her with fear. Thrashing around in her bed, she managed to wake herself before they arrived and sat bolt upright in her bed suddenly. Startled by Sophie's sudden movements, Biggles turned his head towards her and then licked her hand. *We must get to the planet.* Sophie felt an urge to see if she could help with the rocket adjustments.

Jack and Sahil's voices seemed to be increasing in volume as Sophie approached the engine bay.

"So, you say you let the pressure in this chamber expand, but how do you know that is safe?" asked Sahil.

"Because of the release vent. Every chamber has a release vent," replied Jack with a frustrated look.

"But isn't the release vent only able to cope with—"

Jack was losing patience. "Look, Sahil, I know what I'm doing. To teach you everything about rockets would take days. You're just going to have to trust me."

"But I still don't understand how you can be sure that the fuel won't overheat as it bypasses the——"

"Because I've done this 300 times before!" snapped Jack. "Look, I'm going to call the boss; otherwise we will never catch that planet."

"The boss is already here," replied Sophie, who had crept into the room unnoticed.

"Soph, I am sure this thing will work fine, but I'm struggling to convince Sahil."

Sophie could see Jack was getting upset. "Ok, Jack." She wanted to sound professional. "Sahil, what is your concern?"

"I just don't understand one part of it, Sophie. I can't say that it is safe if I don't understand it."

"Jack, please talk me through it," requested Sophie.

Jack let out an exaggerated sigh and then started a long and detailed explanation. Sophie listened intently. She understood most of it thanks to her months of study, during which she had passed several modules on ship's rocket systems. "I think I get it, but maybe if you draw a diagram, it would help?"

Jack sighed again, grabbed a tablet and sketched the rocket system. He then explained his solution more slowly than previously. "Honestly, Sophie, I've done this many times before on other rockets. Yes, this is bigger, but it is also the most solid rocket engine I've ever seen. It will handle it."

"Ah, yes, I see now," said Sahil. "But can I suggest you set up a sensor in this part of the system to record the temperature, which will warn us if there are any problems?"

Jack considered Sahil's suggestion for a moment. "Actually, that's not a bad idea. I'll do that."

Once the adjustments were complete, Sophie, Jack, Sahil, Codey and Biggles returned to the control deck and buckled in. Leena tapped a few buttons.

"Jack, this is good," she said, "you've given me twice as much power."

"It was a team effort, Leena." He nodded at Sahil and then at Sophie before turning back to Leena. "Just don't use all of the fuel because we'll need some later."

"Leena, fire the rockets when you're ready," instructed Sophie.

"Here we go!" said Leena. The rockets boomed, and the kids were pressed hard into the back of their chairs. The ship shook.

"Yeehah!" shouted Jack, cowboy style. "We're coming for you, little planet!"

"Jack, are the rockets ok?" Sophie asked, struggling to make herself heard over the noise. "Yep. I'm watching the temperatures and coolant levels. We're good."

"How long until we're up to speed?" shouted Sophie.

"Almost there," responded Leena, "90%, 95%, that's it!" Leena stopped the rockets. Silence fell.

Leena checked her readings. "Good news Soph, at this speed, we will be approaching the gas planet in four hours, and we've still got quite a lot of fuel left."

"Yeessss!" shouted Jack, punching the air.

Sophie felt a wave of relief. She was pleased with how well they had worked together to keep the mission on track.

"Awesome work, everybody. How about we all celebrate with pizza and chips for lunch?"

The team floated away from their chairs, spun themselves around and climbed down the ladder. They gathered in the kitchen, and Codey started preparing the pizzas.

"Codey, what else do you know how to cook?" asked Sahil.

"I know over 6 million recipes. However, I am programmed to make sure that you eat a healthy diet, so I may have to say no sometimes."

"Can we have brownie and ice cream for pudding?" Sahil asked hopefully.

Codey's eyes flickered, indicating that he was thinking. "Yes."

"Oh, that's my favourite! I love this place!"

After lunch, the children went to their bedrooms to have a rest. Sophie tried to relax, but she kept thinking about how important it will be to take the perfect route past the gas planet. All of the 'what ifs' started to run through her mind. What if they ran out of fuel? What if the engines overheated, or worse, exploded? What if they missed the gas planet completely or accidentally got too close? She didn't want to be the captain of a mission that failed to complete its objectives and disappoint everyone, but she also didn't want to put anyone in danger. This was no longer a simulation. Her decisions really could now kill her crew. *This is what being a leader is all about, I suppose.*

More than this, she couldn't help thinking about her dreams. Something desperately wanted her to get to that planet. Or did it? Dreams are often bizarre. Perhaps it was just her subconscious mind overlapping with events in the real world. Maybe she had just seen one too many sci-fi movies. But, she felt determined to find out. She had to get to the planet.

"Well, all I can do is my best," she said to herself and started writing up some notes to take her mind off things.

A few hours later, Sahil appeared on everybody's communicator. "We are approaching the gas planet. You need to see this!"

They all clambered back up the ladder and floated into the control deck. Sahil had already put the planet on the screen. Sophie gasped at the deep purples, greens and oranges all swirling around. It had a vast hula-hoop of incredible blue rings. They made Saturn's rings look tiny.

"Oh, wow!" exclaimed Sophie. For a moment, she felt hypnotised by the image of the planet. It seemed to stir something deep in her heart.

"Ok, Leena," said Sahil, "I'm sending you the path to pick up as much speed as possible and launch us in the right direction."

Leena replied, "I'm going to need to take us in close. Is everyone ready?"

"Ready when you are, Leena. Just be careful," said Sophie. "Don't be afraid to abort if things get risky."

"Ok. Here goes." Leena grabbed her controller and eased the ship into the path. The planet and its rings grew until they could see nothing else on the main screen. The storms of gases on the planet's surface raged against each other.

Sahil was observing the planet on his screen. "These readings are incredible!" he whispered. He knew he had to let Leena concentrate, but he couldn't keep it in.

Leena gently adjusted the controls, and the ship fired out small bursts of rocket jets, changing direction to keep to the path.

"Coming up to the closest point!" she said.

An enormous cloud of bright orange gas erupted from the surface of the planet and spurted out in front of them.

"Leena, watch out!" screamed Sophie.

Leena pulled back on the controller, and they felt the ship jerk upwards.

"I can't avoid it completely!" shouted Leena. "We'll have to fly through it!"

The ship plunged through the cloud of dust, which battered the hull. Sophie gripped the arms of her seat tightly and clenched her teeth whilst Leena wrestled with her controller, which seemed intent on fighting back.

"Teacup, teacup, teacup," she said quietly. "I have to get back on course."

She lurched the ship downwards and into the cloud. The dust, stones and ice bombarded the ship's hull like hailstones pelting a flimsy plastic roof.

"Keep going, Leena," Jack shouted, gazing at the data on his screen, "the ship can handle this."

Leena forced the controller into position and guided the ship through the gas cloud. Within seconds they were through it and moving away from the planet. She checked the ship's direction. One minor adjustment, and it was perfect.

"Leena, you've nailed it!" yelled Sahil. "You are an awesome pilot."

"Jack, how is the ship?" asked Sophie.

"It looks like only minor damage, nothing that Codey and I can't fix," replied Jack.

"Codey, how long until we get to K2-18b?"

"The gas planet was denser than we anticipated," said Codey. "We've picked up a lot of speed. We should be arriving in 35 days."

The kids all yelled and whooped with relief and happiness. They unbuckled and floated together for a group hug.

"Leena, that was awesome," said Jack as he raised his hand, expecting a high five. Leena failed to respond. "Hey, don't you leave me hanging, Leena!"

Eventually, Leena worked out what Jack wanted. She pushed herself closer to him and high-fived.

"Leena, that was truly incredible flying," said Sophie with a look of admiration. "Just one question, why did you keep saying teacup? Does that mean something else in Finnish?"

"It was something my mum taught me. It's an acronym T – C – U – P. It stands for Think Clearly Under Pressure."

"Leena, I've never known anyone think clearer than you do. Seriously, all of you have done an amazing job so far. I was sitting in my room worrying about everything that could go wrong, but there was no need. This team is brilliant."

"Here, here," replied Sahil in an exaggerated English accent.

So, we've got just over a month until we get to the planet. What do you guys want to do?"

"How about we have some fun on this ship?" suggested Jack.

"Good idea, Jack," responded Sophie. "It's probably about time I did that."

Chapter Eleven
Time for Fun

The kids strolled into the living area and collapsed onto the colourful sofas and bean bags. It had been an exhausting day, but they were too excited to go to bed. Sahil and Jack decided they should have a party.

"Codey, dude!" shouted Jack. "Can you make us, like, a selection of party food and fizzy drinks?"

"Yes, Jack, I will prepare snack platter 1. It has crisps, cheese, fruit—"

Jack tilted his head and frowned. "Crisps? What are crisps?"

"You call them chips in America," replied Sophie, rolling her eyes and smiling at Sahil.

"Wait a minute. In the UK, chips are called crisps?"

"Yeah," said Sophie, "and what you call fries, we call chips." Sophie had learnt this on her holiday to Florida five years ago.

Jack looked as if his head was about to explode. "So chips are, er, crisps and fries are chips?"

"Jack, would you prefer me to switch to a United States dialect?" asked Codey.

"Yeah!" shouted Jack.

"No!" shouted Sophie.

Codey looked between the two children for a moment. "I'm sorry, Jack, but Sophie is the captain. I will follow her instructions."

"Oh, man! The boss wins. Ok, but I'm never gonna get used to crisps and chips."

Sahil was in hysterics. "Jack, so you have no problem with travelling 100 light-years in just a couple of seconds, but you can't get your head around the idea that chips and fries have different names in another country?"

Jack raised one eyebrow at Sahil. "Dude, I used to like you!"

"If this is a party, we should play a party game," said Leena, who showed no interest in the difference between British English and American English. "What should we play?"

"I bet no one has ever played hide and seek in space," said Jack. "This would be another new achievement to add to our list!"

"Jack, we're 12. I stopped playing hide-and-seek a long time ago," replied Sophie in a sarcastic voice.

"You are never too old for hide and seek!" responded Sahil. "I play with my family all the time."

It turns out a spaceship is an awesome place to play hide and seek. On the first go, Sophie volunteered to be the seeker. Biggles followed her around the ship and started sniffing around an air duct. On closer inspection, Sophie noticed the screws had been removed. She knelt, took the cover off and found herself face to face with Jack, who had crammed himself into it.

"Er, hey, boss."

"How did you get in there?"

"It's roomier than it looks. Whilst I was waiting, I adjusted the angle of the vent, making it more efficient," Jack reported with a big grin.

Next, Sophie decided to check the control deck. As she floated in, she was alerted to Sahil's presence not by seeing him but by hearing him giggle. This part of the ship had no artificial gravity, and Sahil's feet appeared from behind one of the control panels.

"Every time part of my body was hidden, the other part just floated out!" said Sahil, laughing.

The enlarged group returned to the lounge area, and they all burst out laughing when they spotted Codey, who was trying to hide behind a chair but was just too obvious. "It appears removing myself from view has not been built into my programming," said Codey.

"We can work on that," replied Sahil, laughing. "I can provide you with better hiding algorithms."

That only left Leena, who was proving tricky to find. After fifteen minutes of seeking together, they felt like they had searched everywhere.

"Where is she?" said Sophie in an exasperated voice.

Codey's eyes blinked. "I have cross-referenced the ship's computer logs with my thermal camera readings. They indicate Leena is hiding in Spacebug."

"Oh, Codey!" exclaimed Jack. "You're not supposed to tell us. It ruins the game."

Sahil laughed. "This is the problem with playing hide and seek with a robot. Too many sensors!"

Sophie laughed. "Sorry, it was my fault. I forgot Codey might take my question too literally. Let's go and get Leena, and we'll have another round."

"Yeah, and this time, Codey, I'm gonna disable your thermal camera and your link to the ship's computer!" said Jack.

Sophie, Sahil, Jack and Codey entered Cargo Bay 3. Biggles trotted in after them, wagging his tail. Sophie opened the rear door of Spacebug and found Leena sitting in the pilot chair, running her hands over the controls. "You won, Leena. We had a little help from Codey."

"Sophie, I love this ship. I can't wait to fly it for real. In the simulator, it was awesome."

"Well, you'll probably get the chance soon enough."

When the children completed a round of everyone seeking, they collapsed into the sofas and started digging into their snacks. Leena, Jack and Sahil were laughing and swapping stories about where they tried to hide.

For the first time in more than two years, Sophie remembered how it felt to relax and be a child again. She had to admit that she thoroughly enjoyed playing hide and seek and couldn't help giggling when explaining how she tried to hide in cargo bay two amongst the food supplies, but Biggles followed her and couldn't sit still with all of the excitement from the smell.

That night they all went to bed tired and happy. After a deep, long sleep, Codey woke them through their communicators.

"Good morning, everyone!" Codey said in his cheerful, robotic voice. "I've made breakfast. It's pancakes with fruit and honey."

The kids staggered out of their rooms in their pyjamas with tangled hair and eyes full of sleepy dust. The smell of the pancakes was wonderful. They exchanged stories over breakfast of their strange dreams.

"I kept dreaming about that gas planet," said Sahil. "I was flying around it just in my spacesuit. It was so cool. Then I woke up thinking I was in my bed on Earth and I looked around confused before I remembered that I'm in a different solar system."

"Me too," said Leena. "When I heard Codey's voice, I thought it was my mum. At first, I was confused why she was speaking English, and then I wondered why she had turned into a robot!"

Sahil laughed as he poured maple syrup onto his pancakes. "Sophie, how did you sleep?"

Sophie's recurring dream had returned and was now more vivid than ever. She had never told anyone about it before, other than her dad via her diary. Remembering her instructions to Leena about being open and honest, she decided to tell the others.

"I've been having the same dream over and over. I must have had it more than twenty times now, but this time it was so intense. I'm always underwater with a creature with yellow eyes. The next moment I'm seeing rocks falling on a strange landscape."

Sahil, Jack and Leena exchanged nervous looks with each other before Jack burst into laughter.

"WoooOOOOoooo! Maybe you can see into the future, Sophie. Maybe we'll all be meeting aliens on K2

18b!"

Jack laughed at himself. Sophie's cheeks reddened as she looked down at her pancake.

Leena noticed Sophie looking embarrassed. "Jack, be quiet. You're such an idiot sometimes," she shouted in her strong, Finnish accent.

"Hey, just joking!" replied Jack as he realised the joke backfired.

"So, what shall we do this morning?" asked Sahil, trying to change the subject.

"What about a game of Football World Cup in the virtual playroom?" suggested Jack.

"You carry on," replied Sophie. "I need to record some more mission observations." Part of her did want to do some more work. Part of her was just annoyed with Jack.

"Come on, Soph," begged Jack, "it would be better with four people."

"No, you guys carry on. I'll see you later." She got up and marched to her room.

Sophie lay on her bed and stared at the ceiling. She was no longer annoyed with Jack but was angry with herself for leaving in a mood. She was happy to hear a soft knock on her door.

"Come in!"

Sophie was surprised to see Leena rather than Jack or Sahil. "Hi, Leena. Are you ok?"

"Er, yeah! I was just coming to see if *you* are ok? Don't listen to Jack; you know he goes over the top sometimes."

"I know, and yeah, I'm fine. Thanks for coming to see me."

"Well, to be honest, I came to beg you to come and play Football World Cup. I think it would be fun."

Sophie thought for a moment and then smiled. "Ok, I suppose I can leave the work until later. But we should all be on the same team so that we work together."

Before leaving, Leena noticed the picture of Sophie's dad. "Is that your dad? Did he work for Space Command?"

Sophie, who had not talked about her father to any of the other children, was surprised by the question. "No, I don't think so. Why do you ask?"

"In the picture, it looks like the conference centre at Space Command. Anyway, see you for the football when you're ready."

As Leena left, Sophie's heart thumped hard. She had stared at the picture countless times over the last two years but never noticed the background. Leena was right; it *was* the Space Command conference centre. No doubt about it. But her dad never discussed working for, or even visiting, Space Command when he was alive, and neither mum nor Dr Millson mentioned this since. *Dad, what did you do for work? And how did you die?*

A mixture of anger and sadness started to bubble up inside her. She stood up and started changing into her sports clothes before it got too far. A good game of virtual football would take her mind off dad.

On entering the virtual playroom, Jack immediately approached Sophie, "Look, Soph, I'm—"

"Jack, it's fine. Let's just play football! You probably call it soccer."

The virtual playroom was the latest in immersive technology. The children slid into special suits, gloves and shoes, which let them touch and feel things in the virtual world that didn't exist in reality. Each of them had an area of moving floor, which meant they could run around without hitting anything, or anyone.

"Ok, team," announced Jack, "let's do this!" He snapped on his headset.

The children were instantly transported into a virtual changing room.

"It feels so real!" exclaimed Sahil. "This is much better than the games I played on Earth."

The game asked them to choose their country. As the children were all from different countries, they decided to be a random country. The computer wheeled through many options before selecting Brazil.

Suddenly their clothes changed into the yellow shirt, blue shorts and white socks of Brazil.

"Oh yeah!" shouted Jack. "Brazil has always been good at soccer!"

The four children and seven computer teammates emerged from the stadium tunnel and lined up to hear the national anthem. The cheerful Brazilian anthem started, and Jack and Sahil nodded their heads, laughing as it played. Then the words came up in front of their eyes.

"Hey, I've learnt some Portuguese!" said Jack. "I had a Brazilian friend at school."

To the dismay of Sophie and Leena, Jack tried to sing along.

"Ouviram do Ipiranga as margens plácidas..."

"Jack, please can we skip this?" begged Sophie.

"I can do it," said Leena, as she pressed the button to start the match.

The referee blew the whistle. Sophie played midfield, Leena positioned herself on the right wing, Sahil was striker, and Jack went in defence. The team worked together, calling each other's names and passing the ball around. Jack got the ball from defence and passed it to Sophie, who kicked it out to Leena. Leena sprinted down the wing with the ball and kicked it as hard as possible into the middle. Sahil's eyes lit up. He scrambled and dived towards the ball, heading it into the top right corner of the goal. The virtual crowd roared. Sahil performed his favourite celebration, which was to dance like a robot.

"Codey would be proud!" shouted Leena.

They continued playing all morning, winning the World Cup twice with two separate teams before stopping for lunch. Codey served pasta to the kids and meaty-flavoured doggy bites to Biggles.

After lunch, the four children pursued their separate interests. Jack checked and repaired the ship with Codey. Sahil performed zero-gravity experiments in the control deck. Sophie got on with her mission observations whilst stroking Biggles, who laid his head on her arm. Leena played a special video game in her room, which once belonged to her great Grandfather and was passed through the family. It was called Space Invaders. She loved it.

As the days turned into weeks, the children developed routines to keep themselves busy. It included playing games, maintaining the ship, exercising, recording video diaries, writing, painting pictures and doing science projects.

Unfortunately for the children, their teachers had pre-recorded more than two hundred school lessons that they could play on their holographic displays. They had agreed to do at least four hours per day, plus homework, although they didn't mind as they all liked studying. After all, every child must do schoolwork, and it reminded them of being back on Earth. They decided to do the lessons together, so it felt more like a classroom. Codey pretended to be the teacher and marked their work.

Sophie felt a deep sense of belonging with her team. The children were sharing more stories of their upbringing and personal lives. Sophie had never discussed dad with anyone her age. She talked to her mum when it first happened, and her auntie and wider family helped at first, but she thought it just made her and everyone else feel sad, so she started to keep it to herself. However, one afternoon the children were telling funny stories about their families. Sahil recounted when his brother got into trouble after hitting a cricket ball through the upstairs window, which shattered glass all over his bedroom and hit him on the head while getting ready for work.

"He then had to go to the office for three days with a huge lump on his head."

Jack failed to contain a mouthful of orange juice as he laughed, which splattered his tablet. Codey brought him a cloth.

Sahil then turned to Sophie. "So, Sophie. What do your mum and dad do for work?"

Sophie swallowed before talking. The pause was noticeable. She hated telling people, but she didn't like to hide it either. "Mum works for an accountancy firm, and my dad died two years ago."

Leena's face fell. Jack looked up from his tablet.

"Oh, Sophie, I'm so sorry to hear that," replied Sahil.

"It's ok, Sahil. You didn't know." Nobody spoke for a few moments before Sophie decided to carry on talking. "It sounds silly, but I speak to him every day in my head. I hear his voice. Sometimes I think he's giving me the determination to try to do something big and meaningful that could help others." Sophie's voice started to break. "I just want to make him proud."

Sahil put his hand on Sophie's arm. "Your dad is proud, Sophie. I'm sure he always has been."

The other children started to tell stories about family members or pets who had died and how it made them feel. Even Leena opened up about how she felt when her grandmother, or Mummo as she called her, died. Although the conversation had turned from fun to serious, the release of emotion made Sophie feel wonderful.

The following weeks flew by. There were some minor disagreements, such as Leena and Jack arguing about virtual playroom time. Sometimes Jack's jokes annoyed everyone, and Sahil's constant talking became too much for Sophie, and she had to bite her tongue to stop herself telling him to just shut up for five minutes. But generally, Sophie had never felt more content.

On day 35, Sophie was jogging around the ship with Biggles when she heard an announcement from the ship's computer that made her heartbeat even faster.

"WARNING. Approaching destination planet. Arrival in one hour."

Chapter Twelve
Arrival

Sophie turned and ran back to the control deck ladder. Sahil was already on the control deck, having spent most of the morning analysing data from the planet. Jack, Leena, Codey and, eventually, Biggles followed Sophie up the ladder.

The planet covered the main screen. It was deep blue with pockets of green and purple. As she floated in front of the screen, Sophie's eyes widened, and her pupils dilated. The goosebumps instantly returned to her arms and neck.

"Sophie, this planet is incredible," said Sahil breathlessly. "I honestly cannot believe what I am seeing. I've been pulling data off the long-range sensors for hours now, and I've double and treble-checked all of the readings and even performed calibration checks on the sensors, and all seems to be correct, but it is beyond my wildest dreams. I can't believe it." He was trembling with excitement.

"Sahil, what is it?"

"Well, I think maybe Jack should check my results. He might also check if I've made a—"

"SAHIL, WHAT HAVE YOU FOUND?" shouted Sophie. The volume of her voice surprised everyone.

"This planet's atmosphere is rich in oxygen. I'm pretty sure we could breathe the air without our spacesuits!"

That nervous, sick feeling was back in Sophie's stomach. Nobody has ever found a planet that humans could live on without spacesuits. She thought about what Dr Millson used to say to her. "The main reason for exploring space is to try to find another planet that could support human life. There are many dangers to humanity if we live only on Earth. There are natural risks, such as huge volcanoes erupting or large asteroids on a collision course with the planet. It was an asteroid hitting Earth 66 million years ago that wiped out the dinosaurs and around three-quarters of all animal and plant life. There are also manmade dangers, such as powerful weapons getting into the wrong hands. We don't realise how fragile our existence is as a single planet civilisation. Having a second home could, one day, prove crucial for the survival of humanity."

K2-18b could be that planet. Sophie told herself to calm down, but butterflies were not just fluttering in her stomach; they were thumping against the sides!

"Not only that, but all those dark blue patches are oceans of water," said Sahil. "This planet is very similar to Earth."

Jack was staring into the image of the planet. "Oh... my...god!"

"But the planet is smaller and less dense than Earth," continued Sahil, "which means gravity is much less. Walking around on the surface will be like bouncing around on a trampoline."

"Even better, I love trampolines!" said Jack. "What are we waiting for? Let's get down there!"

"We need to scan the planet to find a good landing spot," said Sophie.

"I've been doing that," said Sahil, zooming in on a region just about the planet's equator. "I suggest we land here. It looks like the most supportive environment for human life."

Sophie's mouth still hung open as she stared at the planet. For a moment, she completely forgot the procedure for getting ready to descend to the planet surface in Spacebug, despite going through it countless times in simulators. Eventually, she pulled herself together. "Leena, set up the autopilot to keep Flourish orbiting around the planet. Make your preparations, everyone. We'll meet at Spacebug in 30 minutes."

Sophie made her way to her room and started organising her small bag of belongings to take with her. She was still sweaty from running, so she also took the opportunity for a brief shower.

Sophie arrived at cargo bay three to find Sahil and Codey were loading everything they needed into Spacebug, which included Biggles, who had his own chair on this smaller spaceship as well. Jack and Leena were performing pre-flight checks. *It's lucky they all remember what to do*, thought Sophie, who was still thinking about the oxygen and water on the surface. Her mind was spinning when considering what all this might mean when they returned home.

The six of them buckled into the ship, the layout of which was similar to the Flourish control deck but far less spacious. "Opening cargo bay doors," reported Jack.

Flashing amber lights were accompanied by an announcement over the loudspeaker. "WARNING. CARGO BAY 3 DOORS OPENING."

The doors creaked open, and the air rushed out of the cargo bay. They were now looking directly at the planet through the front window of Spacebug. Sophie's hand instinctively lifted to cover her mouth.

She could see the areas of land and sea with her own eyes. It was like a small, more colourful version of Earth, with greens and purples dotted between the swirls of cloud cover. It was stunning.

"Team, this is what we've been waiting for. Is everyone ready to go and explore?"

"Oh yeah, I'm ready, captain," replied Sahil.

"Pre-flight checks complete. Ready, Soph," said Leena.

"Ready, boss," said Jack. "I think I was born for this moment." For once, Jack didn't look like he was joking.

"Leena, take us out."

"Starting engines."

The rockets fizzed into life, firing downwards to lift Spacebug clear of the cargo bay floor.

"Three, two, one, launch."

The rocket jets rotated to shoot Spacebug out of Flourish. Leena gracefully adjusted her controls, and the ship darted left and right. The children were jolted from side to side in their seats.

"I love this ship," whispered Leena.

"We're entering the planet's atmosphere," reported Sahil.

"I'm monitoring the heat shield. All looks good. It won't be long now!" said Jack.

"The planet looks so green!" said Sophie in wonder. "Are they...trees?"

"Yes," confirmed Sahil, almost hopping up and down on his bum with excitement. "I'm detecting huge amounts of carbon-based plant life. Sophie, this is alien life. This is the first time alien life has been discovered anywhere other than Earth!"

"Oh, we are going to be so famous after this!" shouted Jack.

"Guys, calm down. Let Leena concentrate," said Sophie, although her stomach felt like it was about to burst with excitement.

One of Leena's panels started to beep continuously. A large dot appeared on the monitor. "Soph, there is something in our path, but I can't work out what it is. It's moving around!"

"Put it on the big screen," instructed Sophie.

The children were unprepared for what they observed. It appeared to be a blue flying creature.

"Is that a bird? There are birds here!" shouted Sahil. "It's a huge bird!"

"Oh man!" said Jack.

Sophie froze in her chair, staring at the creature on the screen.

"I'm adjusting course to avoid it, but I think there are more!" shouted Leena. She looked increasingly worried as she threw the ship left and right, trying to find a clear route. Suddenly, a flock of large creatures flew out right in front of them. One of them turned and glanced straight at the ship. It was bird-like but had deep blue scaly skin rather than feathers.

"Soph, I've got nowhere to go!" shouted Leena in panic.

BANG!

"We've hit one!" yelled Sahil. The kids were jerked left as the ship jumped right.

"DANGER, HULL BREACH. DANGER, HULL BREACH," announced the ship warning system. Biggles barked furiously.

Jack's fingers started tapping buttons all over his control panel, which was flashing like a Christmas tree. "We've got damage to the main thrusters. We're losing fuel."

"WARNING. FIRE DETECTED IN ENGINE 2."

Sophie flicked her display onto the rear camera, which revealed a trail of flames coming from the ship's rear. "Leena, can you get us down?"

"I have to!" shouted Leena. Sweat was forming on her forehead. She grappled with the controller. "But there's too much forest here. We need a landing area!"

"I've been looking for one, Leena," said Sahil. "Just a few kilometres away is some flat ground. I'm sending you the landing coordinates."

"WARNING. ENGINE 2 IS OFFLINE."

Sophie gripped the armrests of her chair tightly. She didn't want to be the first humans to discover alien life, only to crash and die on impact with it!

"Keep going Leena, you're doing great," said Sahil, who seemed remarkably calm in the circumstances. "We're going to make it to that landing area."

The noise from the engines cut out completely. "WARNING. ENGINE 1 IS OFFLINE."

Leena screamed a word in Finnish that none of them understood. "Sophie, we've lost power! We're gliding!"

"Sahil, how far?"

"Keep going. We should just make it," replied Sahil, checking the distances on the screen.

"Jack, how is the ship?" asked Sophie. He was pressing buttons even more furiously.

"Been better. I'm turning off the voice warnings to let Leena concentrate. We just need to get on the ground."

The next minute or so seemed to last a lifetime. The quietness without the engine noise added to the tension. The only sound was whimpering from Biggles. The clearing was visible on the main screen, but it was just beyond some tall trees. Leena was yanking backwards on her joystick to try to generate lift, but nothing happened. "Sophie, I'm going to hit the tree. I'll aim for the soft-looking bit of it."

"Hold tight, everyone!"

The ship smashed through a tree canopy and spun a full 360 degrees before Leena wrestled with the joystick to stop the rotation. With what little control she had, she glided the ship left and right, narrowly avoiding other thick tree trunks. "Here comes the ground. Brace for impact!"

There was an almighty THUD. The kids were thrown around in their chairs like ragdolls as the spacecraft thumped and skidded along the surface through plants and bushes. Cupboards were flung open, and their contents were thrown around the cabin, banging and crashing as they did. It seemed to take forever for the ship to stop. When it did, the children all looked at each other.

"Is everyone ok?" asked Sophie, gasping for air. She felt something hit her head but couldn't feel any blood.

"I'm so sorry, guys, I couldn't avoid that thing!" said Leena, sweat dripping down her face. After a few more breaths, her face screwed up, and her eyes started filling with tears.

"No one could have expected that," reassured Sophie, "you did amazingly, Leena. You landed us safely with a damaged ship and off our planned course."

"I'm ok," said Sahil, stretching his back and letting out a quiet moan of pain, "and Sophie is right, Leena. Thank you for keeping us alive!"

"I'm ok too," said Jack, who had a trickle of blood coming from his nose, "The damage to the ship is pretty bad, but I'm sure Codey and I can fix that. The bigger problem is our fuel tanks have split, and we've lost a lot of fuel. We won't have enough to take off again."

Sophie took a moment to think about Jack's words and what they meant. *Oh! We might be stuck here. We might never be able to get back home.*

"What can we do, Jack?" asked Sophie, trying to keep her voice calm.

Jack wiped his nose with a tissue. "Well, I'm probably here more for my engineering skill rather than for my personality," he said with a smile. "Let me think about it."

Sahil groaned as he painfully tried to ease himself out of his chair. "Well, Space Command will eventually come looking for us. But it seems we may be here for a while. Anyway, we came here for an adventure. Let's go and explore!"

Codey suddenly beeped into life. "Please stay in your chairs. I need to assess any injuries before you move." His right hand transformed into a scanning device, which whirred as he slowly moved it around Sophie's body.

"What is that, Codey?" asked Sahil. "Is it one of those new, ultralight CT scanners? I was reading about them a few months ago."

"Yes, it is a computed tomography scanner. It uses x-rays to enable me to see inside your bodies to check for internal injuries."

"Shouldn't you start with Sahil?" said Sophie. "He sounds the most injured."

"My protocol states that I must start with the ship's Captain."

"Unless the ship's captain tells you otherwise, I assume? I'm fine Codey, scan Sahil."

Codey paused for a moment. "Ok, I will reorder as requested."

Whilst being scanned, Sahil checked the ship's instrument readings. "All looks good for getting out into trampoline land! The air contains sufficient oxygen and no harmful gases. The temperature is 38 degrees centigrade, and pressure and radiation are within acceptable tolerances for human life."

"38 is hot! It's probably nothing for you, Sahil, growing up in India, but summer in Wales was rarely much above 25 degrees," said Sophie. "How cold was it in Finland, Leena?"

The primary purpose of the question was to get Leena talking, as she was clearly still in shock after the crash landing.

"Er, Finland is cold," Leena mumbled whilst staring into her lap.

Sophie decided that talking about home might help Leena right now. "Where exactly do you live, Leena, and how cold is it?"

Leena lifted her head to reveal her eyes were still puffy and red from her tears. She looked at Sophie and blinked. "I'm sorry, pardon?"

Sophie repeated the question, determined to get her talking.

"I live in the north, near Rovaniemi. In summer, it can be 20 degrees, but in winter, it might be less than minus eight."

"Rovaniemi? I've heard of that," said Jack. "Why would I have heard of that?"

"Well, it is popular for tourists who want to see the Northern Lights. It's also the official home of Santa Claus."

"So that's where you get your flying skills from," joked Jack, "you've been practising with Father Christmas!"

Leena let out a small laugh.

"Oh, Leena, I think we should all visit you when this is over," said Sahil, whilst still being scanned by Codey. "I have never seen the Northern Lights, and I don't think I've ever seen the real Santa Claus!"

"The lights are amazing, although when you see them enough, you get used to them. I think the Santa thing is just for stupid tourists."

The children laughed, including Leena, which pleased Sophie. Unfortunately, Codey delivered the news that immediately forced the mood amongst the kids to come crashing back down.

"Sahil, you have two broken ribs. I would recommend limited movement."

Leena's head dropped again.

"Do you have some device that can heal them up, Codey?" asked Jack, somewhat optimistically.

"No. Ribs cannot be splinted or supported like other bones. They should be left to heal naturally, but we have painkillers in the medical supplies, and we can create a cold compress to reduce swelling."

"Seriously?" replied Jack. "All you can offer poor Sahil is paracetamol and an ice pack?"

"I'll be fine," said Sahil whilst trying hard to avoid showing signs of pain. "And there's no way I'm staying in here the whole time. I have lots of scientific readings to collect."

Other than Jack's nose bleed, Codey reported no other injuries to the children. "Well, that's good news," said Sophie. "Codey, how would you like to try going outside to check the conditions outside?"

"With pleasure," responded Codey. His motors whirred as he carefully stepped through the door to the back of the ship. The door closed behind him. The kids then heard the outer airlock open, and Codey popped up on everyone's communicator.

"What are the conditions, Codey?" asked Sahil.

"Pressure is 869 millibars. I am detecting gases in the following concentrations. Oxygen, 26%, nitrogen, 73%, carbon dioxide, 1.6%, argon, 0.12%—"

Sophie was losing patience. "Codey, can we go out there?"

"All readings are within acceptable risk tolerances for long term human exposure."

"Ok, let's go!" said Sophie.

The children instantly felt the effect of the lower gravity as they unbuckled and climbed out of their chairs. Sahil nursed his ribs as he did so, but he was trying hard not to let the pain show. He swallowed the painkillers provided by Codey with a swig of water from his bottle.

Sophie unbuckled Biggles and led the team into the airlock, a small room to the ship's rear that enabled people to pass whilst keeping the air within the cabin separated from the air outside. Jack closed the door leading to the control deck. It was a bit of a squash with the five of them in there.

"Everyone ready to see the first alien life ever discovered?" said Sophie, with her hand on the lever that opened the large, outside door.

"Oh, yes! This is like a crazy dream!" remarked Sahil.

Sophie was suddenly reminded of her dream but quickly put it out of her mind to avoid distracting herself. She pulled the lever and pushed the heavy door.

The hot, humid air rushed into the ship, and they blinked as the bright light dazzled them. It smelled sweet, almost sickly as if holding a flower permanently to the nose. Sophie took a deep breath. "Well, we haven't suffocated. It looks like Codey was right about the air."

When their eyesight finally adjusted, the view was breathtaking. Sophie poked her head out of the spaceship door. Trees towered above them in every direction, with strange, giant leaves in a rainbow of colours. They looked three times the height of the tallest trees on earth. She stared up into the lush canopies before turning back to her team. "So, who wants to be the first human to set foot on the planet?"

"Me, me, me," shouted Jack. "Please, can I, Sophie?"

Leena was at the back of the group, still with puffy eyes and not talking much. She was still upset about the crash. "Because Leena kept us alive, I think she should lead us out."

"Er, yeah, good idea. I meant to say ladies first. Go for it, Leena," responded Jack sheepishly.

"It's ok, you can go first, Jack," said Leena in a sulky voice.

Jack shuffled himself between Sahil and Biggles and squeezed in behind Leena. "Leena, you have the chance to make history here. Does anyone remember the second guy that stepped onto the moon?"

"Yes, it was Buzz Aldrin," replied Sahil.

"I mean normal people - not space geeks like you, Sahil! Come on, Leena; you're going out first! Sophie's ordered you to."

Jack's upbeat mood cheered Leena up. She let out another small laugh. "Ok, I'm going, I'm going."

Spacebug had cleared a path of flattened foliage as it skidded along the surface. Leena stepped out into it, followed by Jack, then Sahil and finally Sophie. The intense heat made the children's skin tingle.

"This feels weird. I'm going to try to jump as high as I can," said Jack before taking a run-up, planting both feet and leaping as high as he could. For a moment, his feet were as high as Leena's head. "Oh, man! Imagine playing basketball on this planet. It would be super fun!"

"Gravity is just over half what it is on Earth," confirmed Sahil. "This will take some getting used to!" The kids laughed as they bounced around.

Sophie approached Leena and spoke to her quietly. "What do you think?"

"It's beautiful. Incredible," Leena replied whilst staring up into the strange trees. She then turned to look at the damaged ship and then at Sophie. "But how are we going to take off again, Sophie?"

"We'll figure it out."

Sophie turned to Codey, who was also examining part of the broken ship. The sun reflected brightly off his white body. "Codey, how much food and water is on Spacebug?" Sophie asked, squinting.

Codey's motors whirred as he turned and approached Sophie. "Enough for three months," replied Codey, "although by rationing, we could make it last longer."

"Ok, I think we should ration the food immediately."

"Certainly, Sophie. I can control the amount of food you can eat each day. I would recommend reducing food intake gradually, so 80% on day one, then 77.5% on day two, then 72.5% on day three, then...."

"Yes, fine," interrupted Sophie, not wanting to hear the complete day-by-day food intake profile. "How long will it last?"

"Five months."

"That should be more than enough time for Space Command to realise something is wrong and to find us," said Sahil. "But we may also be able to extract drinking water from the environment and even find or grow food."

"Five months?" said Jack sulkily. "This place is nice, but I'm not sure we want to stay for five months?"

"Well, unless you can fix the ship, what choice do we have?" replied Sophie.

Biggles had also emerged from the ship and was sniffing around excitedly and bounding from one place to another. That gave Jack an idea.

"Sophie, if we can find the raw materials, we can probably make some form of rocket fuel. If I let Biggles smell some of the remaining fuel, he can sniff out more of the materials for us."

Eyes widening and face lighting up, Sophie looked genuinely impressed. "Jack, you keep telling us this already, but you really are a genius! Great idea."

"I told you, and I know it's hard to believe, but I'm not just here for my personality!"

Suddenly, a loud squawk from above made Jack almost jump out of his skin. One of the bird creatures swooped over the trees before flapping its immense wings to remain stationary in the sky whilst scanning the landscape. It caught sight of the children and changed direction to head directly towards them.

Chapter Thirteen
Encounter

The enormous flying alien creature squawked and dived straight towards the children at terrifying speed.

"Everyone, back to the ship!" commanded Sophie.

They ran, or rather bounced, back to the ship and scrambled inside. Sahil tripped in panic and let out a cry of pain. Jack helped him to his feet. Sophie was last in and threw the lever to close the airlock door behind her.

Leena put her face close to the side window of Spacebug. "The creature is landing right outside!"

The kids crowded around the window, although it was too small for them all to see out at once. The creature touched down and stretched its wings. It was twice the height of an adult human, and each wing was the length of a bus. "It's more like an aeroplane than a bird. It's huge!" said Jack.

"Of course," said Sahil, still wincing from the pain of his ribs, "gravity is much lower here, but the atmosphere is still quite thick, so animals, birds and even plants can grow much bigger. On Earth, this creature would be too heavy to fly, but here it is no problem."

"So, do you think there could be even bigger animals?" whispered Sophie.

"The land-based animals must be much bigger. Think of how tall a giraffe grows on Earth. In this gravity, a giraffe might grow many times as big."

"Great!" said Jack sarcastically. "Just when we don't have enough to worry about, now we have skyscraper-sized giraffes to deal with."

"Sophie, look at the teeth and body structure," said Sahil. "It must be a plant-eater. I don't think it will be dangerous. Also, it has an injury. The wing is bloody and torn."

"Oh no! That's the bird I hit," said Leena, her face switching from a look of wonder to one of guilt and panic. "That is exactly where I hit it, on its wing."

The creature lowered its head as it looked at the ship.

"Strange, it doesn't look angry," remarked Jack. "It looks kind of sad. Biggles does the same thing with biscuits when he can't have any more."

"Maybe it feels bad for injuring our ship, just as we feel bad for its wing," suggested Sahil.

The giant bird sat and let out a deep sigh from its flaring nostrils.

"I think our new friend is going to stay there until we come out," Sahil observed.

"I want to go out to see if it's ok," said Leena.

"We're all going out," replied Sophie, "but we are going to keep our distance. If there are any signs that it may hurt us, we get back to the ship."

Sophie led the children back to the airlock and opened the door. She poked her head out and looked at the creature. The other three kids all tried to see at the same time and accidentally pushed Sophie out of the door.

"Careful!" whispered Sophie.

The creature lifted its head and looked directly into Sophie's eyes. Then the most extraordinary thing happened, which made Sophie clasp her hand over her mouth. The creature seemed to smile, and not just a slight smile but a big, broad grin.

"No way!" exclaimed Jack.

"No animals on Earth smile, except humans and some monkeys and apes," said Sahil.

"What about dolphins? I've seen dolphins smile," remarked Jack.

"But dolphins are not smiling because they are happy. Their jaw is fixed in a smile shape. I think this thing is smiling because it's happy to see us," replied Sahil.

"It's intelligent!" gasped Sophie.

She approached the large animal. *I wonder if it can understand me,* she thought. "I am Sophie. I am the captain of this ship. We are sorry we hit you when we came into land."

The creature stood suddenly. Leena, Sahil and Jack instinctively backed away. "It's massive!" said Leena. Sophie, who was furthest forwards, stayed where she was. The creature bent its body forward and stretched its neck, moving its head slowly towards Sophie.

"Sophie?" said Leena, nervously.

Rather than feel scared, Sophie felt a connection to the creature. Something profound and calming, as if there was nothing to fear from it. She held up her hand and touched it on the top of the head. The creature made a reassuring purring noise as she continued to caress the side of the enormous head. The skin was rubbery and cold.

"Guys," Sophie whispered, "we are now the first humans to say hello to alien life."

The children all took turns to stroke the creature's blue, snake-like skin. It seemed to love the attention, purring and smiling. Even Biggles, who looked nervous at first, eventually came close for a sniff. The creature seemed to smile more at Biggles than at the children.

Sahil fetched a bottle of water from the ship. "Can I wash your injury there, my friend? It will help it to heal quicker, I think." He squirted the water bottle at the injury and washed the blood away. The creature looked interested in what Sahil was doing but not concerned. "What should we call this species? We are the first to discover it, so we should name it."

"It looks like a cross between a dinosaur and a bird. I'm going to call it dinobird," said Jack.

"It doesn't sound very scientific," replied Leena.

"We're kids; it doesn't have to."

"Good idea Jack," said Sophie happily, "and now we're here I think we should give this planet a better name than K2-18b."

"How about Jack's Planet?" suggested Jack, only half-jokingly. "After all, it was my engineering skill that got us here!"

"And who flew the ship?" asked Leena in an irritated voice. "I don't think you could have done that, Jack."

"True, but without me, you wouldn't have had the rocket power to fly here!" responded Jack.

"Jack, Leena, stop arguing. You're behaving like children!" said Sophie.

"But we are children!" replied Jack.

"Hope!" interrupted Sahil. "Everything about this planet fills me with hope. The fact that there is oxygen, water, loads of trees and vegetation, and now the friendliest animal that I've ever met, other than Biggles. Maybe we can name the planet Hope?"

"I love it," replied Sophie.

"Me too," confirmed Leena.

"Or maybe Jack's Planet of Hope?" asked Jack.

"No!" they all shouted together.

The dinobird started repeatedly moving its head towards its back.

"What's it doing?" wondered Leena.

"Does it have an itch?" asked Jack.

"I think it wants us to climb onto its back. Perhaps it wants to take us for a ride somewhere," suggested Sahil.

"Oh, wow!" exclaimed Leena, "Sophie, can I? I'm the pilot; I should do this."

Sophie considered the tempting possibility of taking a ride on the back of a dragon-like creature, which made the hairs on her neck stand on end, but she remembered what Dr Millson said. "Don't take any unnecessary risks."

"Sorry, Leena, we don't know enough about these creatures yet to let them fly us around."

The dinobird looked thoughtful. It then squawked and took off, blasting the kids with a gush of wind from its broad wings before flying straight up, glancing at the children, smiling again and disappearing over the tall trees. Staring in silent wonder, the children got lost in their thoughts for a while.

"So, what are we going to do about Spacebug?" asked Leena, eventually breaking the silence.

Everyone looked at Sophie, who took a moment to formalise a plan in her head. "Ok, Jack, Codey and Biggles, why don't you go and look for the materials you need to make more rocket fuel. Meanwhile, Sahil, Leena and I will start preparing food and a camp for the night."

"You got it, boss. We can keep in touch with the communicators. Codey, can you keep an eye out for any huge creatures that might eat us?" said Jack.

"Yes, Jack. My thermal camera can detect lifeforms even through the thick forest," responded Codey, failing to realise it was a joke.

Jack pulled a handkerchief from his pocket and soaked it into a puddle of fuel that had leaked from the fuel tank, and then let Biggles sniff it. "We need more of this, boy. Good boy!" He patted Biggles on the head.

Biggles wagged his tail and bounced off towards the forest, sniffing the air as he went. "Woah! Wait a minute, boy." Jack grabbed a backpack from the ship, threw some supplies into it and bounded after Biggles, trying to catch up with him.

Codey followed. "See you later, guys!"

Biggles led the three of them into the dense forest.

Chapter Fourteen
Bad News

Sophie considered their situation. If Jack failed to fix the ship, the only hope of getting home was to await rescue. There was no way of telling how long that might take, but she was sure it would be months. Again, her thoughts turned to her mum, who would be worried sick when they failed to return on time.

Stay positive, Soph. The good news was the planet seemed to have everything they needed to survive a long time. Their discoveries were going to change everything. Humans had long wondered if there was other life in the universe, and Sophie and her team were the first to discover it. It was their duty to collect as much scientific data as they could. However, they were still just four kids who now faced many months alone on an alien world with just a robot, a dog and a small, battered spaceship. This had not been part of the plan.

Stay positive, Soph. If dad was here, what would he say? Be calm. Think logically. Don't waste energy worrying about things you can't change. Focus on what you can do. I wish he were here now! But he's not, so I better just get on with it.

"Leena, Sahil, I think we can build a structure onto the side of Spacebug that gives us a much bigger living area. We can set up hammocks for beds, which would be more comfy than sleeping in Spacebug, and we can build a dining table in the middle."

"Perfect! I'll find some wood to build with," responded Sahil, with his typical child-like enthusiasm. "This will be fun."

"I'll get the tools from Spacebug," said Leena.

The three children decided to start with the table, which was probably the easiest thing to build. They tied logs together with vines and made two benches to go either side. Working in the heat was exhausting. Sophie handed out water, which they sipped whilst admiring their work.

"I wonder if we are the first to build furniture on this planet," said Sahil, laughing at himself.

Sophie sat at the table and caressed it with her hand. "You know, it's pretty good. Perhaps we can set up a shop for the locals!"

Leena didn't look amused. Something was on her mind.

"What is it, Leena?" asked Sophie.

"What if we can't fix Spacebug?"

"Space Command will come looking for us."

Leena's eyes turned angrier. "But how long will that take?" she snapped.

Sophie decided honesty was the best approach. "Ok, let's think it through. Space Command may take up to two months to realise something is wrong when we fail to return on time. They will then launch a rescue mission, but there is always the possibility of hyperdrive problems or anything else going wrong when they come to this star system. They will then need to find us on the planet, which they can do by listening for Spacebug's transmission, but it may not be easy to land nearby in dense forest. It may take a while."

Again, Sophie started thinking about her mum being alone and how she might cope. Her feeling of guilt returned, flooding her stomach. After longing to go into space for so long, she was starting to wish she was back home. She imagined mum's cheerful smile and the smell of her cooking.

Leena seemed to notice Sophie's change in mood, and she put her hands to her face, covering her eyes.

Moments later, her body started shaking, and Sophie realised she was crying. "Se on minun syytäni," she mumbled to herself.

Sophie went round to Leena's side of the table and put her arm around her. Despite not speaking Finnish, she suspected she understood what Leena had said. *It's my fault.*

"Leena, we are alive, and that is thanks to you. It's not your fault. Look at me. It's not your fault."

Leena sobbed into Sophie's shoulder, which Sophie knew was a good thing. It was bad to keep emotions bottled up. After a few minutes, Leena's tears stopped, and she wiped them away.

"I'm sorry, Sophie. I know I should be stronger than this."

"It's better to let your emotions out than to keep them—"

Sophie's communicator pinged, interrupting her flow.

"Sophie!" whispered Jack.

"Sophie!" he repeated, in a slightly louder whisper, and with panic creeping into his voice.

The screen was black, and Jack's voice was barely audible.

"Jack, what is it? Where are you?"

Jack was breathing unnaturally fast. "I'm st-stuck. There's a big...thing...outside. Sophie, help!"

"Jack, calm down. What's happening?"

"We w-were walking through the forest when Codey d-detected a h-huge lifeform. It had eight legs and was the size of a h-house. Soph, it's like a massive sp-sp-sp—."

Oh no. Sophie knew he was trying to say spider and that this was not one of Jack's terrible pranks. He was petrified.

"Where are you now?"

"I found a c-cave, and we dived in. Sophie, it's just outside! I can see one of the hairy legs!"

"Is Codey and Biggles with you?"

"Yes. I'm trying to keep them both quiet."

"Ok, stay where you are, Jack. We have your location from the communicator. We will come and get you out of there. Just stay calm."

Sahil was listening wide-eyed and open-mouthed. He picked up his electric saw and started sharpening some sticks into spears. "Sophie, I think we should take these, just in case."

"Why don't we just use the electric saw as a weapon?" asked Leena.

"A spear just seems more, I don't know, appropriate," replied Sahil.

"If there is one thing Space Command mission planners failed to consider," Sophie said, "it was weapons to defend ourselves against giant alien spiders! Ok, let's take the spears and some supplies and go and find them."

Running around desperately trying to think what else they should take with them, Sophie started to wonder what else could go wrong.

What if we get lost? I'll take food and water.

What if the temperature drops at night time? I'll pack some blankets.

What if we get attacked? Medikit.

Emerging from Spacebug with a backpack crammed full, she felt thankful that gravity was much lower as it would have weighed far more on Earth.

"Ok, come on, we will follow the trail and use the coordinates...."

Her voice trailed off as something emerged above the trees that caught her eye. Her mouth fell open. Sahil and Leena turned to look. A flock of dinobirds made a series of squawks as they glided straight towards the children. The kids froze.

"I count eight of them!" observed Sahil.

Leena looked confused. "What's on their backs?"

As they flew closer, the children observed human-shaped creatures riding the dinobirds. The eight bird-creatures circled and glided down to land nearby. The humanoid beings dismounted. They had long, thin arms and legs with scaly skin like the dinobirds, but it was apricot-pink rather than blue.

The Hopian people strode towards the children, with one of them leading the other seven. Up close, the size of the creatures became clear. They were each around three times the height of the children. Each alien was bald, with what Sophie assumed were nostrils for breathing located towards the outside of their heads and a small mouth directly in the centre of the face. Then, Sophie spotted the eyes. Deep, yellow eyes with a small black slit. Her own eyes widened even further. *My dream. This is the creature in my dream.* Previously, the alien had always been blurred by the water, but it was definitely the same type of creature. Her breathing quickened as she started to realise what this meant. Her dreams were not random. They had meant something.

The leader stared down into Sophie's eyes and tilted its head to one side. Sophie's heart was thumping hard.

"Sophie!" whispered Leena, her voice full of nerves.

What came next took them entirely by surprise. All eight Hopians knelt and bowed their heads towards the floor.

"This must be their greeting. Quick, copy them!" commanded Sophie, and the three of them tried to imitate the action.

The Hopian people stood on their thin, spindly legs. The leader continued to look at Sophie.

Sophie wondered if they could understand English. In her dream, the creature had spoken to her in English. *But that was a dream.* She didn't expect them to, but it seemed appropriate to try. "My name is Sophie. I'm captain of this ship. We are from a planet called Earth." She cringed at what she had just said. It sounded like it came from a cheesy, old sci-fi movie.

The Hopian people looked at each other. The leader started to make clicking noises. It was directed at the other Hopians at first, and then it was clear they were trying to talk to the children.

"How are we supposed to understand them?" asked Leena.

Sophie tried a simpler message. Patting her chest, she slowly repeated a single word. "Sophie."

Again, the leader just looked, although there was the slightest sign of a smile as the small mouth curled up at the sides.

Come on. You know me. You've spoken to me many times.

"We need to find a way of communicating," said Sahil. "I've got an idea." He ran into Spacebug and returned with a pen and notepad, which he put on the new table. "I always keep these in case my tablet fails me."

Sahil gestured to the Hopian people to come closer, which they did, towering over Sahil. He then sketched the Earth, stick figures of the four children, Biggles and Codey getting on a spaceship and then onto Spacebug, hitting the dinobird and crash landing. Sahil drew slowly, taking care to get the details right. "I'm trying to do it like a comic book, to tell the story."

"Sahil, this is excellent," said Sophie.

As the Hopians looked down at Sahil's masterpiece, they started clicking and whistling excitedly to each other.

"Sahil, I don't believe it. They understand. This is amazing," said Sophie, laughing in disbelief. "Continue drawing, Sahil. Draw Jack, Biggles and Codey looking for fuel and with the spider."

"Luckily, I've always been good at art as well as science!" responded Sahil, and he sketched Spacebug losing its fuel and then Jack, Codey and Biggles searching for more and a spider approaching them. He put the pen on the table. "We need to look for them!" he said, trying to indicate the meaning with simple sign language.

Again, the Hopian people talked with each other. The leader slowly reached forward with its long, webbed fingers. It picked up the pen and held it in front of its face, investigating it closely.

"Come on. Draw us something," whispered Sophie.

To Sophie's delight, the Hopian lent forwards and made a mark on the paper. It was just a line at first, but it was a start. The first page was a mess of scribble.

"Do you want to try a new page?" offered Sahil, slowly tearing the previous one away.

The Hopian slowed down the drawing action and drew a circle, and added patterns on top. Next came dots spread around it.

"It's this planet!" said Sophie. "It's drawing Hope."

"This is amazing," said Leena.

Next to the planet, the Hopian drew a jagged shape, followed by a line that started at the new shape and approached the planet. As the line reached Hope, the Hopian scribbled furiously. The leader looked to the sky with a frown. All of the other Hopians also looked sad.

"What does this mean?" asked Leena anxiously. "Sophie, Sahil, what does this mean?" she asked again, her voice growing louder and angrier.

Sophie's heart sank. As she looked into the drawing, she was terrified that she knew what it meant. "Sahil?" she said in a slow, quiet voice.

"Yes?" he replied equally slowly, his expression suggesting he knew something was deeply wrong.

"Do you have a way of checking for meteors heading for this planet?"

Sahil looked at Sophie, back at the drawing and then at Sophie again. He jumped up from the table and raced back into Spacebug. Sophie and Leena followed. Sahil started tapping at the controls.

"I'm linking to Flourish and gathering information from the long-range sensors. We should be able to do a full sweep of incoming objects within the...Oh no."

"Sahil, what is it?"

Sahil tapped more buttons. "No, this can't be right. One second."

"SAHIL, what have you found?" shouted Sophie, panic searing through her voice.

"There is a huge meteor heading directly for this planet! It is a rock over 100km in size. Sophie, if this thing hits Hope, nothing here will survive."

"How long until it hits?" asked Sophie.

Sahil tapped several more buttons. "Well, if the velocity is accurate, and according to this reading, I think I've got it to within a 10% confidence level, and assuming...."

"SAHIL, HOW LONG?" screamed Sophie.

"Just over 30 hours. I think."

Sophie closed her eyes.

"Sophie, what are we going to do?" asked Leena.

Sophie kept her eyes closed, desperately trying to think things through. *Come on, work the problem.* The problem was, she had nothing. There was no solution to this. It was her turn for the emotions to boil over. She opened her eyes, which were now filling with tears, and looked back at Leena. Her bottom lip was quivering. "I don't know."

A sudden feeling of despair washed over her. Every negative emotion rushed through her mind. How could she be put in charge of this mission and have no idea what to do? How could she have discovered life, only for it to be wiped out, with her new friends, straight after? How was mum going to survive being left all alone?

"Oh, Sophie," said Leena, her own eyes filling with tears again. She hugged Sophie.

Sahil was still tapping buttons on his screen. "Yes, it's definitely going to hit, but it's more like 31 hours."

"Great, thanks, Sahil!" replied Sophie sarcastically, which made Leena laugh a little. "Come on, let's go back outside."

The Hopian people were waiting for them. Sophie looked up at the leader. She didn't know what else to do but offer a hug and opened her arms. The Hopian seemed to understand, knelt and embraced Sophie. The skin of the Hopian leader was cold but comforting. As their heads touched, Sophie recalled her dream. "Either I can dream the future, or you've known about this for a long time," she whispered into the leader's ear, "and you wanted us to come and save you. I think it's the latter. How did you get into my dreams?"

The Hopian looked into Sophie's eyes with a knowing expression but didn't talk. It then stood and gestured for the children to ride with them on the dinobirds.

"Well, I suppose we can risk it now!" said Sophie.

Chapter Fifteen
Flight

The thought of riding on the back of the dinobirds filled Sophie with both excitement and terror. There was no choice now. The clock was ticking, not just to find Jack, but to see if they could save themselves and maybe even the Hopians from the destruction of the meteor. The vision of her dreams prompted a wave of shivers through her body. The raining molten rocks. The fire. The destruction. It was a vision of hell.

She decided to check if Jack was ok and to tell him about the meteor. He might have ideas on what to do. Her communicator lit up with a tap. "Jack? Jack, come in, over."

No response.

"Jack, talk to me!"

Still nothing.

"JACK?"

Sophie's raised voice attracted the attention of Sahil. "Maybe he's lost signal."

"Or he's too scared to answer," suggested Leena.

"Or something's happened to him," replied Sophie as she screwed up her face and rubbed her forehead with her hand. She instantly regretted what she said. Speculating about what may have happened was the last thing she should be doing right now, and it was up to her to show positivity, although she wasn't feeling much right now. "Come on, let's get on these birds and go find him."

The Hopian leader brought the dinobird to Sophie. It ambled along, wobbling its bum, and then lowered its head so its neck was level with Sophie's waist. Sophie jumped and hoisted her leg over, attempting to grip the rough, scaly skin. The birds had tentacles coming out from just behind the neck, which made convenient reigns. Sophie noticed the Hopians holding them earlier, so she grabbed them. The leader climbed on behind and also gripped the tentacles with arms on either side of Sophie's body. The dinobird raised its head, causing Sophie and the Hopian to slide backwards. It was like the Hopian leader was cuddling Sophie which, although it was purely for practical purposes, felt nice.

Two other Hopians did the same for Sahil and Leena. Sahil mounted awkwardly whilst Leena jumped on in a flash. The twinkle of confidence had returned to her eye.

The birds flapped their giant wings, took off and climbed just a few metres. Sophie felt her body sliding to the right and gripped the left tentacle as hard as she could. The creature's muscles flexed up and down to beat the mighty wings, and Sophie felt it was only a matter of time before she would fall. As she got used to the pattern, she started shifting her weight left and right to adapt. Typically, Leena looked comfortable from the first second and was even smiling. Sahil was anything but comfortable, and on a down flap, almost slipped off the creature completely. His accompanying Hopian grabbed his arm and pulled him back on.

The Hopians seemed to be waiting for the kids to get the hang of staying mounted before the leader let out a series of whistles. Suddenly all of the birds rose together until they were above the trees.

"Oh, my goodness!" shrieked Sahil. "Sophie, we are very, very high!"

Trying to avoid looking directly down, Sophie looked to the horizon. The whole landscape of planet Hope came into view. In the distance, there were towering mountains before they rolled away into vast lakes and oceans. The vivid greens and purples of the forests made Sophie forget, for a moment at least, about the danger the planet was in, the danger Jack was in, or even the danger she was now in riding on the back of an alien dragon.

She checked Jack's location on her communicator and pointed. "That way!" The birds flapped their broad wings and gracefully soared over the trees.

"Well, we came here for adventure!" Sophie shouted to Leena and Sahil as the birds picked up speed.

"This is the most amazing thing I have ever done!" shouted Leena, the wind whistling through her ponytail.

Sophie had to agree. If they lived to tell the tale, what a tale it would be! *Would anyone even believe them?*

The view was so mesmerising, Sophie almost forgot to check her communicator for the location. Holding on even harder with one hand, she used her other to tap it and realised Jack was just a few metres ahead.

"Down!" she shouted to the Hopian leader, whose head was just above and slightly behind her own. Remembering that English was no use, she risked letting go with one hand again so she could point directly downwards.

The leader shrieked and whistled, which the dinobird seemed to understand as an instruction. It circled down towards the tree canopies and then dived straight through the narrowest of gaps between the large branches. It collided with a few smaller ones, which shed a bunch of leaves. Sophie gripped tighter than ever as the leader ducked just above her. The dinobird found barely enough space to open both wings but still managed to touch down gently. The other seven birds performed similarly impossible-looking manoeuvres.

Catching her breath, Sophie jumped off and checked her communicator. *No time to lose.* She bounded over the vegetation towards the flashing dot on her watch, which was now less than 30 metres ahead.

"JACK!"

The foliage was thick, but Sophie just pushed her way through. Branches scratched her face and arms. As she emerged on the other side, she got the fright of her life. Her feet gave way on the loose surface whilst trying to skid to a stop, and she fell onto her back. It felt like time had slowed as she found herself face to face with the creature.

The first thing she distinguished was the face. The head was enormous, and the jet-black eyes were looking straight into hers. Large fangs were sticking out from the sides. Each leg looked like a thick stem of bamboo that lifted the body to the height of a two-storey house. A long tail with pincers was raised above the head, making it look more like a scorpion than a spider.

The head lowered towards Sophie, who was paralysed. It was typical in these situations for the body to enter 'fight or flight' mode, which means either preparing to fight back or to run away. She could do neither. She was in *fright* mode. She had never felt smaller and weaker, and having fallen onto her backside, she was in no position to run. She tried to shout to warn the others, but even her voice failed her.

The giant arachnid continued to lower its head closer to Sophie's, to the point where she could smell its breath. It was like rotten fish. The mouth then started to open. "No!"

She had heard stories of people's lives flashing before their eyes when close to death, but all she could think of was her mum. It wasn't fair to leave her alone. Again, the guilt at wanting to go to space returned. Mari knew how dangerous it was. *That's why she cried when I first told her about the mission. I've messed up.*

"SOPHIE!" shouted Leena, emerging through the bushes. She then yelled something in Finnish when she glanced at the creature. To Sophie's amazement, Leena threw her arms up and ran towards the spider, screaming at the top of her voice. "GET AWAY FROM HER!"

The spider raised its head to look at Leena and then tilted it to one side. *Oh no! It's now going to attack Leena,* thought Sophie. Only, it didn't. The spider took one step back. Then another. It looked confused and slightly scared. Leena had made this giant creature, which was about ten times her height, back off.

The Hopian leader emerged through the foliage, followed by Sahil, who stared up at the spider open-mouthed. Calmly, the Hopian strolled over to the spider, reached up and touched its forehead with one hand. The spider shuffled its long legs and laid down like a well-trained dog that had just been instructed to do so.

"They can talk directly to the creatures," said Sahil in a wondrous voice.

Leena helped Sophie to her feet. "Are you ok, Sophie?"

"I am, thanks to you!" Sophie replied.

Rechecking her communicator, Sophie looked in the direction of Jack's signal. The entrance to a cave was barely visible amongst the vegetation. Sophie approached it, more cautiously than before, and then pushed some vines aside and climbed in.

"Jack?"

The cave was pitch black. Compared to the humidity outside, it was cool and damp. The rocks were slimy as Sophie felt her way along them, and then she heard something running fast towards her. It was another creature of some kind. Still on edge after the spider incident, Sophie's heart began to thump in her chest once more. The creature jumped up at her and pushed her backwards. Sophie screamed, slipped on the wet rocks and fell onto her bum, sending a surge of pain through her coccyx.

She tried to activate her communicator to call for help, but in panic, failed to find the button. The creatures breath smelt a bit like that of the spiders, but there was a wet nose sniffing around her face. *Wait a minute. That nose feels familiar.*

A bristly tongue licked her cheek. "Biggles?"

Reaching into the darkness, her hand was met with warm, soft fur.

"Oh, Biggles. I am so happy it's you."

She put her arms around him and pulled him close for a hug. Biggles made a whimpering sound as if to complain about leaving him in this cave.

"Where's Jack?"

A dim light was coming from the end of a narrow passageway. She winced with pain as she stood up and continued along wall towards it. Rounding a bend, she found Jack sitting next to Codey. His hands were shaking, and he was drenched in sweat.

"Jack, it's ok. They've sorted out the big spider thing."

Jack was trembling and staring straight ahead.

"JACK! It's me, Sophie. You're ok!"

Jack suddenly looked Sophie in the eyes and blinked. "S-S-Sophie?"

"Yes. The spider has gone, Jack. You're safe." She leant in and hugged him.

"Sophie, it was s-so...big."

"I know. But it's out of the way now."

Sophie looked at Codey. His eyes lit the otherwise dark cave. "Are you ok, Codey?"

There was no reply.

"Codey?"

Still nothing.

"Ah, it's ok, Codey, you can speak now," said Jack.

"Thank you, Jack. Apologies Sophie, Jack instructed me not to make a sound. There was no time frame attached to his instruction, so I was waiting for permission. Yes, my systems are operating perfectly."

Jack and Sophie laughed, which started as a chuckle and then erupted into hysterics. It was a welcome release of emotions.

As the laughter died down, Sophie's expression turned more serious. "A lot has happened since we last spoke." She told Jack the story of the Hopians landing, the drawing and Sahil detecting the meteor.

"No way! What are the chances of us landing on a planet just 30 hours before a mass extinction event? It must be millions to one!"

"I'm not sure it's a coincidence," replied Sophie.

"What do you mean?"

"Nothing, it doesn't matter." Sophie didn't want to waste time speculating about her dreams and whether the Hopians had used them to contact her. "What can we do, Jack?"

"We must find fuel. If we can take off, maybe we can intercept the meteor."

"Come outside and meet the Hopian people."

Sophie helped Jack to his feet, and the two of them walked hand-in-hand out of the cave. Jack was still shaking slightly, but he was much better than before. Codey and Biggles followed them.

They emerged from the cave, and the leader was waiting for them, alongside Sahil and Leena.

"Jack, meet the Hopian leader," said Sophie.

Jack looked straight ahead and then slowly upwards towards the face of the Hopian. "Er, hey!"

The Hopian leader smiled at Jack. Biggles bounded around sniffing, and one of the other Hopians seemed very interested in him. Biggles approached and licked its scaly leg, which was all he could reach. The Hopian made a series of whistles that sounded a bit like laughter.

Jack gave a hug to Leena and then to Sahil. It felt good to all be back together again.

"Okay, everyone," said Sophie, keen to come up with some kind of plan, "this is the situation. In around 30 hours, the meteor will strike. We must find something we can use as rocket fuel and take off. If we can..." Sophie became distracted by the Hopian with Biggles, who was kneeling and touching Biggles' head with its own.

"What's it doing?"

Jack turned to look. "Maybe it wants a cuddle with Biggles."

It then stood up decisively and spoke to the other Hopians. Immediately, they gestured to the children to get back onto the birds.

"I wonder if they've managed to work out what Biggles is thinking," said Sahil. "They may be telepathic, which means they can read minds! It seemed to be what they did with the spider, and now it's working on Biggles."

"And Biggles knows what rocket fuel smells like!" exclaimed Sophie, her eyes lighting up. "Come on, let's go!"

Sophie, Leena and Sahil started to climb onto the backs of the birds.

"Sophie, I have not been programmed to ride one of these creatures," said Codey, which was his way of saying he had no idea how to do it.

"None of us have either," responded Sophie with a smile, "but it's quite easy, just hold on tight."

"Are you sure about this, Sophie?" asked Jack.

"We can trust them now, Jack," responded Sophie. "And we don't have much time, do we? Just get on Jack, and try to, er, stay on!"

Biggles hopped onto the back of one of the dinobirds and was joined by his new best friend, the Hopian.

"Look, if Biggles can do it, then I'm sure you can," said Sahil, laughing.

Leena brushed past Jack on the way to her dinobird. "You're going to love this!" she said with a wink.

Jack looked up to the Hopian, who seemed to be offering him a ride. "Ok big guy, I guess I'm with you. Let's do this!"

Jack climbed onto the back of the dinobird, which stood and lifted his feet off the floor. The sudden movement made him slide to the right. He grabbed a tentacle to stop himself from falling.

"Woah! Easy there. I'm a first-time flyer!"

Jack's Hopian partner then acrobatically vaulted onto the dinobird from behind, landing behind Jack and crashing into his back in the process.

Jack turned and looked up at the Hopian with annoyance. "You know your leader was a lot more gentle with our boss! Maybe you could learn something."

Before Jack had turned to face forwards again, the dinobird stretched and flapped its giant wings, lifting him 20 metres into the air.

"Woah, hey, no, no, get me down, I wasn't ready!"

Sophie, Leena and Sahil laughed at Jack as their own dinobirds lifted them. "Jack, stop complaining and enjoy the ride!" shouted Leena.

The Hopian with Biggles clung onto him tightly and seemed to be enjoying the cuddle. Biggles wagged his tail.

Codey's head darted quickly in all directions as his dinobird lifted him off the ground. "Are you ok, Codey?" shouted Sophie.

"I believe so, Sophie," he reported back. "I'm calculating the force of grip needed to maximise the probability of staying on the back of this lifeform. My sensors, actuators and gyroscopes are all functioning optimally, and my...."

"Just 'yes' is fine!" Sophie shouted.

The group of dinobirds with their new passengers continued flying directly upwards to clear the trees before the Hopian leader let out a stream of whistles. The birds lunged forwards and raced over the mountains and rivers, hills and valleys.

Sophie caught sight of something out of the corner of her eye. Other flying creatures were joining them, flitting around between the flock of dinobirds. Some looked like pterodactyls but were much larger than those that lived on Earth millions of years ago. There were smaller birds, large insects and things that looked a bit like giant butterflies. It was as if they sensed something was happening and wanted to be involved.

"Look over there!" yelled Leena, pointing towards a clearing. They glanced down to see a herd of unbelievably tall animals with extensively long legs and necks, as if someone had stretched a giraffe to five times its standard height. The creatures looked up at the children and smiled.

"Everything here looks so friendly!" shouted Sophie.

"I just hope we can save them from the meteor," responded Sahil.

Chapter Sixteen
New Mission

The wind whistled through Sophie's hair as her dinobird raced over the lush, colourful landscape. She squinted into the distance. Tall, rectangular shapes were emerging on the horizon. When they got closer, she realised they were buildings. "It's a city!" she said to herself. "We're flying into an alien city!"

The buildings were all shapes and sizes, but the majority were made from glistening deep purple stone and were separated not by roads but by rivers that flowed in a very controlled way between them. It reminded Sophie of her family trip to Venice a few years ago. As the dinobirds circled over the city, Sophie spotted Hopian people swimming along the rivers.

"This must be how they travel around the city!" yelled Sahil. "They don't use roads and vehicles. They just swim!"

The Hopian leader stretched her arm out in front of Sophie and pointed, encouraging her to look in the other direction. There were large green areas that looked like parks with neatly arranged trees, fountains and big lakes. Smaller versions of the Hopian people, about the size of a grown-up human, were smiling and playing, taking it in turns to do somersaults into the lake, and gracefully swimming to the other side. "Hopian children!" she shouted. The others looked over.

Sophie thought about the meteor again. *We must save them.*

The dinobirds continued over the city and headed towards a blue, rocky mountain with gaping holes in its side.

"This looks like a mining area," shouted Jack. "It must be where they get their building material."

The birds touched down and lowered their bodies so that the children could jump off. Jack stumbled as he did so and then leant forwards with his arms on his waist, breathing heavily. "I think I'm going to be sick."

"Why are we here?" asked Leena. All of a sudden, Biggles started jumping around, barking and trying to dig.

"They've found the rocket fuel!" said Jack, in between deep breaths. "Codey, are you able to dig down where Biggles is?"

"Yes, Jack. Digging to collect rock samples is one of my primary functions," he said as he held up his hands. His finger motors whirred as they folded into his arms, and out came pieces of material that transformed into a shovel and a pickaxe.

Codey just stood, looking at Jack, who then realised his instruction wasn't explicit enough. "Start digging, Codey!"

Codey whirred his arms around and attacked the rock and soil below him. In no time, he was about a metre down. "Testing the material." Codey used his built-in chemical sensors. "Confirmed as Ammonium Potassium Nitrate."

"That could work!" said Jack. "Let's get this back to Spacebug, and we should be able to turn it into rocket fuel."

The children and Hopians all helped gather the material. They loaded it into sacks and containers and strapped it to the dinobirds. The team, which now included four children, one dog, one robot, eight Hopian people, eight giant bird creatures and several other flying alien things that seemed curious about what was happening, took off and raced back to the ship.

On the way, Sophie thought about the following key steps. She was relieved they had a plan to save her team from the meteor by taking off from the surface of the planet, but she still didn't know how they were going to stop the meteor from hitting Hope. She thought about what Jack said. 'Intercept the meteor'. *What did that mean exactly?* She needed to talk it through with him.

The dinobirds glided down to the clearing and landed next to Spacebug. They all dismounted and looked at Sophie expectantly.

"Jack, it's time for you to do your magic. If ever we needed a good engineer, it's now! I suggest you take charge to get everything ready for take-off."

"Ok guys, listen up," said Jack, enjoying the attention. "It will be quicker if we work together on this. There are multiple fractures of the ship's hull. Sahil, grab the welding kit and start repairing the cracks. Leena, check the sensors and see if they need replacing. Sophie, you can test the electrics. Meanwhile, Codey and I will start synthesising the rocket fuel."

The Hopians watched curiously as the children got busy. If anything, they were working too quickly. Sahil burnt his wrist on the welder. Jack accidentally splashed rocket fuel in his face. Sophie almost electrocuted herself by failing to disconnect the power to the wires, which sparked in front of her. Leena slipped off the roof of the ship whilst checking a sensor.

"Everyone, just calm down!" shouted Sophie. "Yes, we've got to do this quickly, but we've got to get this right, otherwise..." She decided not to finish the sentence.

After two hours, all four children were dripping with sweat. Jack was doing final checks. "Soph, we're ready to launch."

"Ok, everyone, we can't waste any time but let's say a quick goodbye to our new friends," Sophie said. She hoped it wouldn't be the last time she saw them. Each Hopian knelt to hug each of the children. Sophie gave an extra long hug to the leader. "We will do our best to save your planet," she whispered.

The children strapped themselves into Spacebug. "Leena, take us up," instructed Sophie.

"Three, two, one, launch," exclaimed Leena, without delay.

Sophie kept her fingers crossed that the rocket fuel and the repairs would work. The rockets started to fire, and the Hopians backed away. To Sophie's relief, the ship began to lift.

Leena was repeatedly tapping buttons and moving her joystick. "Soph, somethings wrong. We've got no power."

The ship hovered a few metres off the ground before falling back down with a thud.

"Try it again," said Jack.

Leena repeated the exercise, but the same thing happened, although the ship only reached a metre or so off the ground this time.

"No, no, no, NO!" shouted Jack. He banged his fist on his control panel.

"Jack, what's happened?" asked Sophie, trying to remain calm.

"We did the best we could to make the fuel, but it doesn't have the energy density. It's working, but it's not giving us enough power to escape the planet's gravity. I was worried this might happen."

Biggles let out a whine as the kids sat in their chairs, looking at each other. No one knew what to say. Sophie felt the emotions bubbling up inside of her. Not now. *Don't cry now. Come on, Sophie, be a leader and find a solution.*

"Shall I try it again, Sophie?" asked Leena nervously.

"No, it's not going to work. We might break the ship even more," replied Jack with his head in his hands.

Sahil kept looking as if he had an idea, but just as he was about to speak, he shook his head and whispered, "No, that won't work."

Well, this could be it, thought Sophie. *Unless someone comes up with something, we will soon be destroyed along with everything on this planet.*

Suddenly, there was a knock on the airlock door. Sophie unbuckled and went to open it. The Hopian leader was outside and gesturing for her to come out. Sophie didn't feel like trying to communicate what had happened. *What can I say? What picture can I draw to say sorry, your world is going to end soon, and there is nothing we can do?*

But, to Sophie's surprise, the Hopian grabbed Sophie's hand, pulled her over to the table, picked up the pen and started to sketch something.

"Sahil, Leena, Jack, get out here!" shouted Sophie. "I think *they* have an idea."

The children gathered around. The Hopian leader's purple tongue poked out the side of its mouth as it concentrated on drawing an oval on the page.

"It's our ship!" observed Sahil.

Above the ship, the unmistakable shape of a dinobird was emerging. Its feet were connected to the top of the ship.

Sahil gasped. "They are offering to lift us off the ground. Jack, if they can fly us a few hundred metres up, would we have enough rocket power then?"

Jack's eyes widened. "Woah, that might just work if they can fly us fast enough." Jack looked up at the

Hopian leader with his hand outstretched. "Wait a minute, big man, give me the pen!"

"Jack, I don't think the leader is male," stated Sophie.

"How do you know, Sophie?" asked Sahil. "I was looking for signs of reproductive organs, and I couldn't see any."

"Sahil, dude, you're weird," said Jack.

Sophie ignored Jack's childish comment and responded to Sahil. "I don't know why but I get the feeling it's a she. I'm feeling some kind of, er, connection. I'm sure it's a female."

Jack started drawing logs bolted to the ship for the dinobirds to grip. "We've got eight dinobirds, and we are going to need all of them to help lift and fly as fast as possible." He added the additional seven dinobirds holding onto the logs. "If we design it right, the dinobirds can release us, and then we fire the rockets which will burn through the logs."

The Hopian leader looked at Jack's drawing and then directed some clicking noises towards two of the other Hopians, who immediately mounted their dinobirds and took off.

"Hey, where are they going?" asked Jack. "Sophie, what did your alien queen ask them to do? We need those dinobirds, and we need some big wood, quickly."

"I don't know Jack, but I'm sensing she has a plan."

"Well, I hope this connection of yours is working, and she's not completely misunderstood the problem!"

A few minutes later, the kids all looked up at the same time, mouths wide open. The two Hopians on the dinobirds had returned, but it was what followed them that stunned the children. The heads of four of the enormous giraffe creatures emerged from over the trees. Each was the height of a ten storey building. The four towering creatures were working in pairs, each carrying a long tree log in their mouths. They gently lowered them down next to the ship.

Sophie, who moments ago was in the depths of despair, felt overwhelmed with joy at the sight of these majestic beings helping them. "Thank you!" she shouted, waving up at them. Each of them produced big, friendly smiles before turning away.

"Looks like those skyscraper giraffes can be very useful!" said Sahil.

Jack just continued to stare at them with his mouth open. It was like he was frozen. "Jack, let's go!" shouted Sophie.

With Codey's help, the children built the wooden framework for the dinobirds to grip and bolted it onto the ship. They then strapped themselves in for a second time. Each of the eight Hopians mounted their dinobird and moved into position, ready to take off.

"Leena, don't fire the rockets until we're as high as they can take us," Jack instructed.

Sophie watched out of the window as the Hopian leader gave her command, and the dinobirds started flapping. The strain in their faces was unmistakable. The Hopian people whistled excitedly to encourage the birds. Slowly but surely, the ship began to lift.

"It's working!" shouted Leena. "We're lifting."

Once the ship was off the floor, the birds started to gain momentum. The children gazed out of the spaceship windows as they were raised above tree level. The giraffe creatures were walking away and turning to look back at them.

"When should I fire the rockets?" asked Leena.

Sophie watched the dinobirds and the Hopian leader closely. After gradually accelerating, they suddenly started to beat their wings furiously. This seemed to be their absolute top speed.

"NOW, Leena!" shouted Sophie.

The rockets spluttered into action as the dinobirds let go.

"Give it full power!" ordered Jack.

"I am!" yelled Leena.

"It's working," said Sahil, "we're continuing to climb."

The rear-facing monitor confirmed that they were flying upwards. The rockets burnt through the logs, which fell to the ground. The Hopians, dinobirds and giant giraffes were looking up at them before quickly getting smaller and disappearing from view.

Sophie closed her eyes and let out a huge sigh.

"I knew we would do it," joked Jack. "I don't know what everyone was getting so worried about!"

Sahil and Leena giggled.

Sophie gave him an evil glare before smiling and shaking her head. "Ok, Mr Genius Engineer, what are our options for saving Hope?"

"Well," started Jack, "in the movies, they would just fly up to it and blast it with their laser cannon."

"But we don't have laser cannons," Sophie reminded him in a sarcastic voice. "We don't have any weapons."

"No, I know," continued Jack, "but we do have rockets. All we need to do is land on the meteor and blast our rockets to change its path. With a little push, we should be able to make sure it misses Hope."

"Sahil, Leena, what do you think?" Sophie asked.

"Yes, it should work," confirmed Sahil. "To be honest, I don't think we have any other option. But it won't be easy landing on the meteor!"

"And, unfortunately, the rockets on Spacebug will be too small. We will have to land Flourish on it," said Jack, looking apologetically towards Leena.

Leena's eyes widened as she turned to Jack. She then looked back at her control panel and was noticeably quiet. Her earlier smile had disappeared.

Two minutes of awkward silence followed until, eventually, Leena turned around. "Sophie, I've never landed something like Flourish on a meteor before. I don't know if I can do it."

"I know, Leena. Don't worry. We will work it out together, somehow," Sophie reassured her. "One thing at a time. First, let's get back to Flourish."

Chapter Seventeen
Leena's Training

Leena flew Spacebug back into Flourish's cargo bay, and they closed the airlock. The team made their way back to the control deck.

"Leena, how long will it take to get to the meteor?" asked Sophie.

"I've plotted a path that will take 15 hours," said Leena.

"Ok, let's go," instructed Sophie. Leena's hands tapped the controls. Flourish's smaller rockets fired to turn the ship around before the main thruster blasted them away from Hope and towards the meteor.

Sophie was considering how difficult it would be for Leena to land a ship the size of Flourish on a tiny meteor. It would be like trying to land a jumbo jet in a back garden. The more she thought about it, the more her mind raced. From nowhere, her dad's voice popped into her head. "Failing to prepare is preparing to fail." He must have said that to her thousands of times. She now needed to follow that advice more than ever.

"Sahil, how much can you detect about the meteor from here?" Sophie asked.

"Our long-range sensors can get a pretty good idea of its size, shape, density, what it is made from, how fast it's spinning. Everything, really," replied Sahil.

"Leena, I've got an idea. If Jack, Sahil and Codey can build an exact simulation of the meteor and this ship in the virtual playroom, would that help you practise the landing?"

Leena's eyes lit up. "Yes, yes, yes. Sophie, that's a brilliant idea. I can practice all night until I get it perfect."

"Jack, Sahil, can you do it?"

"This will be the best land-a-large-spaceship-on-a-small-rock simulator anyone's ever built! Well, best and only!" said Jack, and the three of them immediately headed off to start coding it.

Sophie and Leena were alone with Biggles on the control deck. Sophie could tell Leena was nervous.

"Leena, I know you want to save the planet as much as all of us, but if you think this is too risky, please tell me."

"I will, Soph," responded Leena with a small smile.

Sophie ordered Leena to get something to eat and then go and rest. After grabbing a quick sandwich for herself, Sophie made some for the boys and headed to the virtual playroom. Jack and Sahil were working hard with Codey to prepare the simulator, tweaking small parts of the programme to make everything as realistic as possible. Jack was testing it when Sophie arrived.

"Sahil, the chair doesn't feel like this. It's not this soft! Can't you make it harder? And some of these buttons are in the wrong place."

"Really? I'm just trying to get the details of the meteor right!"

"But we've got to make everything as realistic as possible! That includes the chair and the controls."

"Ok, ok, give me a minute. Going into the chair design now. How is this?"

The virtual chair under Jack's bottom suddenly switched to solid metal. "Too hard!"

"Ok, try this," said Sahil, tapping a few more buttons.

"Nope, too soft again."

"Is your name Goldilocks? Ok, how about this?"

"Ah, just right."

The boys' discussions were escalating into full-blown arguments about the most trivial details. Sahil looked exhausted. "Jack, I think we should just let Leena practice now! Honestly, it's as good as we can make it."

"I agree. Honestly, I think it looks excellent," said Sophie, tapping her communicator. "Leena, come and see what you think."

Leena entered the virtual playroom and put on her headset. "Guys, this *is* perfect," she said as she looked around. "It looks identical to the real one in Flourish."

"Well, we will leave you to try it," said Sahil. "The meteor is spinning quite fast, but I know you're a great pilot, Leena, so see what you can do."

Sahil, Jack and Codey left the playroom. Sophie stayed to see Leena's first attempts and offer moral support.

Leena took the controls and put the meteor up on the screen. "Sahil was right when he said that thing is spinning fast!" she said. She manoeuvred the ship into position and tried to match the spin of Flourish to the spin of the meteor. She attempted to touch down.

BOOM! The virtual ship vibrated suddenly.

"IMPACT SPEED TOO HIGH!" reported the simulator in a harsh, computer voice.

"Ok, try again." She tried a slightly different approach angle and tried to match the spin of the ship to the meteor. This time the ship collided with another part of it.

BOOM! "IMPACT SPEED TOO HIGH!"

Leena took a deep breath. "It's going to be a long night."

"Take your time Leena. I'll let you practice alone."

Sophie went outside but continued to watch Leena on a monitor. Despite two hours of continuous practising, it wasn't going well. Out of 56 attempts, not once had Leena managed to land the ship on the meteor. She decided to go in and talk to Leena.

Leena pulled off her headset. "Sophie, it's just spinning too fast, and this ship is too big!"

"Leena, you are the most amazing pilot I've ever seen, but what you are trying to do is unbelievably difficult. Try not to get frustrated."

Leena was avoiding eye contact with Sophie. "I know. It's ok."

Sophie was not in the mood to accept that as a response. "Leena, look at me."

Leena's eyes darted to either side, and then, finally, they met Sophie's eyes. Sophie could see the stress in them. "This is not the time to keep things inside. Please tell me what you're thinking. You must let me help you deal with this."

"It's just..." Leena's voice began to break, and her eyes glazed over. "I don't know what to do. I keep thinking about all those creatures on the planet. The dinobirds, the Hopian people, the Hopian children! I don't want to let them die!"

"Leena, it would not be you letting them die. If we weren't here, they would have died anyway. There is a small chance that we can save them, but if we can't, it will not be your fault!"

Leena broke down in floods of tears. The two girls hugged. Biggles came in and licked Leena's hand. Leena buried her head into Biggles's soft fur.

Sophie could see Leena was exhausted. It had been an incredibly long day, and she wasn't sure if it was supposed to be day or night anymore. "Look, we still have 12 hours until we reach the meteor. Go and get some sleep, Leena. Sometimes, problems are easier to deal with after a good sleep."

"But, I don't know if I can get to sleep thinking about all this."

"Just try, Leena. You're going to need to concentrate later, but you must be rested."

"But..."

"Leena, go!"

Sophie was tired also, and she didn't intend for her instructions to sound quite so bossy. Before she had a chance to apologize, Leena had gone. *Oh, well,* she thought. *I'm going for a lie down as well.*

Back in her room, Sophie's head hit the pillow, which felt wonderfully soft and comforting. Her heavy eyelids fell shut, and then she drifted off. Twenty minutes passed in what seemed like seconds to Sophie. The beep of her communicator woke her. Leena's face popped up. Her eyes were puffy and red.

"Leena? What is it?"

Leena was breathing unnaturally quickly. "Sophie, I'm sorry, but...you told me to tell you what I'm feeling. All I can think is how am I supposed to sleep with all this happening? I need to save the planet, and I need to practice!"

"Wait there. I'm coming to your room."

Sophie hauled herself up and scampered along the corridor to Leena's door. It slid sideways, and she went inside. Leena was sat on her bed with her face in her hands.

"I can't stop thinking about the meteor, Sophie. I still don't know if I can do it. But I have to do it. But I just...I can't get the approach right, and if I mess it up, it could..."

Leena looked terrible. Her eyes were darting widely from side to side as she struggled to express herself clearly. She then paused, took a deep breath and looked straight at Sophie. "If I get this wrong, it will not only destroy Hope. It will kill us, Sophie."

Sophie sat on the bedside chair and took Leena's hand.

"Leena, I know. But that's not for you to worry about. I'm the captain, so let me worry about that. All you need to do now is sleep." Sophie remembered tips her dad used to tell her. "Lie down and close your eyes."

Leena did as instructed.

"Take some slow deep breaths. Breathe with me – in for 1, 2, 3, 4, 5, hold for 1, 2, and out for 1, 2, 3, 4, 5. Keep doing that. Slow, deep breaths."

Leena was already starting to calm down. Sophie could tell her heart rate was slowing. "Now you need to picture yourself somewhere relaxing. What kind of place do you find relaxing?"

Leena opened her eyes. "But, how will this help with..."

"Please, just trust me, Leena. Close your eyes and tell me about a place you love to be."

Leena closed her eyes again and thought for a moment. "Well, there is one place I love. When we go on family holidays, we always go to the same place, and there is a hammock overlooking the beach. I love that hammock."

"Good. So, imagine yourself rocking in the hammock. You have your eyes closed. What do you hear and smell?"

"I hear the waves breaking gently against the sand. My young cousins are normally there, and I hear them playing and laughing. I hear my parents and my auntie and uncle laughing. I can smell the salty sea. I can...I can..." Her words faded and were replaced by light snoring.

Sophie smiled and glanced up to the ceiling. "Never fails, dad," she whispered. Then she gently released Leena's hand, tiptoed out the room and went to use the same technique on herself.

Six hours later, Sophie got a ping on her communicator. It was Leena, looking infinitely better. She was bright and alert. "Soph, I've got an idea!" she said with a smile.

Sophie sat up in bed and blinked at the bright light from her communicator in her otherwise pitch-black room. Leena's words felt like part of her dream, but she soon realised she was now awake. She tried to disguise a yawn. "What is it, Leena?"

"I need to slow it down! I was trying to match the approach to the spin of the meteor, but it was spinning too fast. If I fire the rockets at one end first, I can slow it down!" Her voice was brimming with confidence and enthusiasm.

"Leena, that's brilliant. Let's go and try!"

Sophie jumped out of bed and dashed to the simulator. Leena was already there and snapped the headset on. "Which game would you like to play?" asked the computer in a soft female voice.

"Meteor Landing v1.9," said Leena. Instantly she was in her virtual pilot seat, grabbing the controls and steering Flourish towards the meteor, which she had now done many times before, but this time she kept her distance and watched how the rock was spinning. She tapped some buttons and pulled back on the controller to move Flourish's main thruster close to one end of the meteor before giving the rockets a short blast. "It's working!" she said to herself. "The spin is slowing!" One more blast, and the meteor's spin slowed even more. A few more button taps lowered the landing pads and positioned the ship close to the meteor surface. It was now much easier to keep everything under control. She held her breath and eased her lever forwards. The ship jolted.

"TOUCH DOWN SUCCESSFUL."

Chapter Eighteen
Real Thing

Leena and Sophie embraced after the successful meteor touchdown in the simulator. They both agreed that Leena would continue to practice but with plenty of breaks for rest and food. They started with breakfast.

After several hours, Leena was getting more confident about landing on the meteor. Sahil and Jack were feeding the simulator with more accurate information about the exact size and spin.

With less than two hours to go until they arrived at the meteor, Sophie instructed everyone to meet in the lounge.

"Ok, everybody," Sophie announced, "I want to be clear about what we are going to try to do. The plan is to try something that I don't think anyone has ever tried. We are going to attempt to land a large spaceship on a small meteor. We will then blast the rockets to change the path of the meteor. There is a chance we can save Planet Hope, and all of the intelligent life that we know lives there."

Sophie's voice turned more serious. "But there is also a chance that we could crash and die. Today in the simulator, Leena landed successfully 183 times and crashed 28 times. We also know that real life is never quite the same as it is in simulators."

Sophie paused to give each of them a chance to think. "I want to tell you that we still have a choice. We could choose to go straight back home to our families. Nobody would feel bad if we made this choice. It is probably what Dr Millson would be telling me to do right now. Or we could carry on and try to save Hope."

Sophie pulled a bag and some coloured pieces of paper out of her pocket. "I don't want anyone to feel pressured into choosing the option they don't want, and everyone has to agree to take this risk, so we are going to do secret votes. I'm going to give each of you a blue piece of paper and a green piece of paper. If you want to go straight back to Earth, put the blue piece of paper into the bag. If you want to try to land on the meteor, put the green piece of paper into the bag. We will then look in the bag. If there is a single piece of blue paper, then we are going straight back to Earth."

In silence, every child slid a piece of paper into the bag without showing the others which choice they had made. Sophie opened the bag and pulled out the pieces of paper. The other three children stared intensely. In all the months they had been together, they had never felt like this.

Sophie opened her hand. All four pieces of paper were green.

"Yes!" shouted Sahil, unable to contain his emotions a moment longer. Jack sighed in relief. Leena showed no emotion and just stared at the paper.

"Ok, let's do this then!" said Sophie.

Leena completed five more successful practice landings in the simulator before heading to her room to relax.

"Ok, it's time!" said Jack over the communicators. "We will be with the meteor in 20 minutes." The team gathered on the control deck and buckled up. Leena came in last.

"Are you ok, Leena?" asked Sophie.

"Yep, I've got this," confirmed Leena. She gave Sophie a reassuring smile. "Jack, give me full control of the rockets."

"Switching rockets from autopilot to manual control," said Jack.

Sahil was tapping his leg up and down and looking increasingly fidgety. Sophie knew this meant he was nervous. "What's wrong, Sahil?"

"Sophie, we are just picking up new readings from the short-range sensors. The meteor is much denser and heavier than we previously detected. It's because we previously thought it was 75% silicate, but actually, it has a lot more iron hidden deeper in the—"

"Sahil, what does this mean?" interrupted Sophie.

"Well, the simulation assumed that the density of the meteor would lead to an angular velocity of—"

"SAHIL! GET TO THE POINT!" shouted Sophie, unable to hide her impatience any longer.

Sahil dropped his head. "I'm sorry, Sophie. Our simulation was wrong. Very wrong."

Sophie's heart sank. "Can we delay the attempt?" asked Sophie.

"No," shouted Jack. "We have planned the course to intercept on this approach. We won't have enough fuel if we don't land now."

The three children stared at Sophie, waiting for her instructions.

"Soph, I could just try it?" Leena offered in a shaky voice.

Sophie was looking down into her lap before letting her eyes close. She had to think fast. It was now too risky. But what could she do? After a few quiet moments, something inside suddenly snapped her into action.

"Jack, Sahil, how long would it take to update the simulator with the new readings?"

"Just a couple of minutes," responded Jack, "but Sophie, we—"

"Do it!" instructed Sophie in a firm voice.

"But Sophie, there's not enough time to—"

"DO IT NOW!" shouted Sophie. Sahil jumped. Jack looked shocked. They both unbuckled and scrambled to the virtual playroom as ordered. Sophie turned to Leena whilst tapping her communicator so the others could hear the instructions.

"Leena, we have just over 18 minutes. You are going to spend 3 minutes telling me how to start the approach to the meteor. It will take 1 minute for you to get to the simulator, and I then want you to practise for 9 minutes with the new settings. Land as often as you can within that time. With 5 minutes to go, get back here, and we decide whether to land."

"Got it," responded Leena.

Leena explained as clearly as she could what Sophie needed to do to slow the ship to the correct speed and start the approach. Luckily, Sophie had undertaken the basic pilot training at Space Command. This was just refreshing her memory. Leena scuttled away to the simulator whilst Sophie moved to Leena's chair and started easing the ship into position.

"Sahil, Jack, report!" said Sophie over the communicator.

"Just a few more adjustments, and, ok, it's ready," said Sahil.

"Good. Leave the channel open so I know what's happening."

"Sahil, fast forward to the final approach!" said Leena. Sophie could see her fiddling with the virtual controls and blasted the rocket jet to slow down the meteor spin.

"It's not working; the spin is still too fast. Rewind to the starting position! Ok, I'm trying at a different angle. No, that's worse." She screamed a swear word in Finnish.

Meanwhile, Sophie was finding it tough to control the ship. She was approaching too fast. "Jack, get back here and give me a hand!"

Seconds later, Jack emerged at the top of the ladder and glided to a position where he could look over Sophie's shoulder. "Try a quick burst on the front thrusters. I'll stabilise using the side rockets."

The two worked together to maintain a good approach. Leena was on her sixth attempt but couldn't find a way of slowing the meteor enough.

"Two minutes left in here," advised Sahil.

"Ok, seventh attempt," reported Leena. "I'm going to give the meteor more of a blast. It's looking better. Attempting landing."

"TOUCH DOWN SUCCESSFUL."

"Do you want to try one more time?" asked Sahil.

"There's no time; let's just go and land this thing!" said Leena.

Within seconds, Leena emerged onto the control deck. Sophie vacated the pilot's chair for her. "Leena, are you sure you want to do this?"

"Yes."

"Good luck."

Leena strapped herself in and tapped some buttons, and moved her control lever gently. She positioned the rockets exactly as she had practised on the last attempt and fired them at the meteor.

"It's working," said Sahil. "The angular velocity of the meteor is now—"

"Be quiet," said Leena, tapping further buttons.

The small rockets fired to match Flourish's spin to that of the meteor. The ship and meteor were like ballet dancers, harmonising perfectly as they hurtled through space. Leena pulled a lever to lower the landing pads. Sophie had never witnessed such intense concentration.

Pushing the lever forwards, Leena went for a landing. "No," she muttered under her breath and jerked the controller back to lift the ship. Sophie's stomach felt like it would descend through the bottom of her chair as the ship lurched upwards. Leena repeated this four or five times. Sweat dripped from her forehead, and she had to pause to wipe it from her eyes.

Sophie tried to hide the fact that she was terrified. She could do nothing but keep quiet and let Leena concentrate.

Leena eased her control lever forwards. It was looking good. It had not looked better. She was going for it and pushed the lever down further. The spaceship jolted with metallic THUD.

Jack checked the readings on his screen. "Leena, you've done it!" shouted Jack. "We're on the meteor!" Leena's eyes rolled straight up to the ceiling, and she let out a sigh. She glanced at Sophie.

"Leena, you are a superstar!" said Sophie. "Ok, let's push this thing well clear of Hope."

Leena fired the rockets directly upwards for a few minutes to push the meteor onto a new path.

"That should do it," said Sahil, "there is now no chance that this rock will hit Hope. It will fly straight past and will burn up in the star."

"Guys, we have just saved an alien planet."

"Woohooo!" shouted Jack. The four of them floated together and embraced. They held each other tight as the four of them rotated in zero gravity.

"Thank you, everyone. I'm sorry if I was bossy," said Sophie, mid hug.

"Sophie, you were awesome!" replied Jack.

"Absolutely," responded Sahil.

Leena's eyes had filled with tears again. "Thank you, Sophie," she whispered.

"So, what now, boss?" Jack asked.

"We need to make one last visit to our new friends before we go home," replied Sophie.

Chapter Nineteen
Party Time

Sophie wanted to make sure the Hopians knew the meteor had been diverted to avoid the possibility of apocalyptic panic within the alien world. The Hopians had the technology to detect the meteor in the first place, but she wasn't sure if they would have seen Leena's heroic landing, which nudged it away from a collision course with Hope.

Whilst waiting to arrive at Hope, the kids were still buzzing from the excitement. They celebrated by playing Ice Skating Disco Party in the virtual playroom. Leena was an excellent skater. She spun and twirled and was equally comfortable gliding forwards or backwards. Sophie was competent and had mastered going fast but fell when trying anything fancy. Jack and Sahil spent most of their time either clinging to the side or lying on the ice, but they had fun anyway and improved towards the end. Jack then decided to stop skating and take over as the DJ.

"Hey, Jack, can you show me how to do that?" asked Leena.

"Yeah, but I don't think you'll be as good as me," replied Jack. "I have decks a bit like this at home."

"You're forgetting, it's a machine."

Much to Jack's annoyance, and Sahil and Sophie's amusement, Leena was a much better DJ. The kids danced on the ice as Leena seamlessly mixed one dance song into another with perfect timing and an equally impressive light show. It was the best skating party they had ever experienced.

A while later, they approached the orbit of Hope and headed for Spacebug, which Jack and Codey had now properly repaired and refuelled. Sophie buckled Biggles into his seat whilst the others took theirs. Codey docked himself.

"Initiating launch," Leena said. "Everyone look for dinobirds this time. I don't want to hit another one!"

"Maybe they will be looking out for us now," suggested Sophie. "Leena, take us towards the Hopian City."

The rockets fired, and Spacebug zoomed out of Flourish and towards the planet's atmosphere. The planet was mostly clear of clouds, which made the blue, green and purple surface colours even more vibrant.

"I can't believe we managed to save this planet from being destroyed," said Jack, a tear running down his cheek.

Codey looked at the tear. "Are you sad, Jack?"

"No, Codey, I'm happy. Very happy. Sometimes happiness also makes us cry."

The ship headed towards the city.

"I'm detecting dinobirds and other creatures," warned Sahil, "but this time they are flying in some kind of formation. Sophie, you were right; they have seen us coming."

A flock of dinobirds and a selection of other flying creatures approached and started to fly alongside Spacebug. The creatures were every colour of the rainbow. Some were butterfly-shaped, some were insect-shaped, some were bird-shaped. Some were like nothing on Earth.

"They were waiting for us," said Sophie. "I think they are guiding us down to land."

Leena adjusted her controller to take her place in the formation just behind the lead dinobird. They followed closely, flying low over the city towards a central square where it looked like they were expected to land. The square was surrounded by masses of Hopian people.

Sahil looked out of his window. "Oh my goodness. There are thousands of them!"

Leena lowered Spacebug into the centre of the square. The hum of the rockets was replaced by a chorus of whistles, cheers and clapping from the waiting crowd. Sahil switched the view to the main display. Row after row of Hopians were jumping wildly with their arms in the air.

"It looks like they've realised what we've done!" said Jack.

"I think this will be another first," remarked Sophie, "the first party between humans and aliens!"

The four children, Biggles and Codey headed towards the door of Spacebug. They could hear the celebratory whistles and cheers growing louder. Butterflies were again fluttering inside Sophie's tummy, but this time it was pure excitement.

"Right," said Sophie, taking a deep breath, "here we go."

She pushed the button to open the door. The bright light flooded in, and the roar was deafening. It was a sea of tall, thin, reptile people. All of them were grinning, clapping, cheering, whistling, dancing and jumping. The team set foot on the Hopian surface once more and were approached by the leader. She marched towards Sophie with a broad grin and her reddish-pink arms outstretched, knelt and embraced her. The Hopian whispered some noises into Sophie's ear. Sophie guessed it meant thank you. "You're welcome," she replied.

The Hopian then gestured to the other team members, and they joined the hug. Leena's emotions bubbled over, and tears of happiness flowed.

Codey seemed to have learnt that he should join in. He wasn't sure how to hug a tall Hopian that was four times his size. He extended his legs to match The Hopian's size, but that just scared the Hopian backwards.

Biggles spotted the Hopian that he had made friends with previously and bounded over to it. He leapt incredibly high in the low gravity, and the Hopian caught Biggles in its arms. Biggles licked its face. The Hopian giggled excitedly.

Sophie looked into the crowd, spotted a Hopian child and approached it. "Hello, I'm Sophie," she said with her biggest smile. The Hopian child looked up at what must have been its parents. There was a frantic exchange of clicking, and then the Hopian child opened its arms to Sophie. The child was about as tall as a grown-up human, so it was easier to hug than a grown-up Hopian.

Jack was enjoying himself, waving, dancing and saluting. He gestured to a section of the crowd to raise both arms as he ran past, and repeated this until there was a wave of thin, Hopian arms flowing, like the type of wave that entertains crowds at sports events.

"Jack, have you just taught aliens how to do a Mexican wave?" shouted Sahil in disbelief.

"I think so!" yelled Jack, with the biggest grin.

Sophie observed everyone having fun, but she knew they couldn't stay long. They were trained to visit the surface of a planet and collect data on what exists, but not to be the first to have long conversations between themselves and an alien species. That would need careful thought and was a job for politicians, not explorers, and especially not child explorers. She was happy that the Hopians knew the meteor would miss them, and they were not panicking. They were celebrating. Now was a good time to get home and report back to Space Command. The team headed back to Spacebug, turned and waved to the crowd for a final time.

Sahil closed Spacebug's door, and everything fell much quieter. The kids all looked at each other and burst out laughing. "That was the most awesome thing I've ever done," said Jack.

"I have a funny feeling this will not be the last time we see the Hopians," said Sophie. "Let's get back to

Earth. We've got quite a lot to tell them about!"

Chapter Twenty
Reporting

The team returned to Flourish, and Jack and Codey started preparing the hyperdrive to jump back to Earth's solar system. Sophie floated into the control deck. The main screen displayed a beautiful view of Planet Hope. She reflected for a moment on what they had achieved. *I'm sure dad would be smiling if he could see me now.*

She had mixed feelings about returning home. Of course, she could not wait to see mum again, but how could she return to her everyday life after what she had experienced? How could she sit in one of Mr Galway's English classes and deal with the boredom of learning the names of different types of verbs after saving a planet full of intelligent alien life from certain destruction?

Her bigger worry was whether she would ever get the chance to return to Hope. She thought about the friendships they had developed with the creatures and the deep connection she felt with the Hopian leader.

And then there was her dream. Had the Hopian leader actually communicated with her? The Hopians were certainly telepathic, but how would she communicate over such a distance? Surely, that would be impossible.

Or was it a vision of the future? A premonition, which would have happened if they had not stopped it? That seemed equally unlikely. Sophie didn't believe in mystical powers. No one can see the future. If someone could, they would be prolific lottery winners!

Or was it just a coincidence? But that seemed as unlikely as the first two theories. She considered the shape of the Hopian leader's head. The yellow eyes. The effects of the meteor. Maybe one of those things could be a coincidence, but not all three.

The more she thought about it, the more she convinced herself that the Hopian leader had somehow entered her dreams on purpose. *But how?*

Sophie's communicator beeped, and Jack appeared on it. "Okay, boss, the hyperdrive is good to go."

The team assembled on the control deck and strapped in.

Sophie glanced around at her crewmates. She felt infinite respect and love for each of them. "Are we all ready for this?"

"I'm going to miss this place!" said Sahil. "Sophie, do you think we will be able to come back?"

"I hope so! But let's enjoy some rest and time with our families. I think we deserve it! Leena, activate the hyperdrive."

The wormhole opened with the same thunderous crack. The ship whooshed into it whilst the hyperdrive engine hummed. As the ship shook, the kids felt their organs were trying to escape from their bodies whilst the light from thousands of stars flashed at the windows. The feeling of lunging through the wormhole was no less intense this time around, but they knew what to expect, so it didn't feel as scary as the first time. They emerged on the other side.

"Where are we?" asked Sophie whilst trying to recover from the jump.

Leena checked her readings. "We are between Earth and Mars, just a few days from Earth."

"That's a relief," said Sophie, aware their previous jump took them a long way off course. "The ship will immediately be sending information from our trip back to Space Command, but we all need to write up our reports of our experiences."

The children went back to their rooms and worked on their reports. Sahil prepared scientific observations, Jack focussed on engineering, Leena wrote about her piloting endeavours, and Sophie produced mountains of papers on what had happened with the creatures of Hope and the meteor.

Codey popped up on everyone's communicator. "We are receiving a video call from Space Command."

The team rushed to the control deck. The light flashed, and Sophie knew it would probably be Dr Millson popping up on the screen as soon as she pressed the button, and her hand began to shake. Would Dr Millson be angry that she took too many risks? Sophie was well aware that they all could have died on this mission and were probably lucky to be alive. She took a deep breath and tapped the button.

Dr Millson appeared in front of hundreds of grown-ups at Space Command. "Flourish, this is Space Command. Are you receiving?"

Sophie responded as professionally as she could whilst trying to keep her emotions under control. "Space Command, this is Flourish, we are receiving, over."

With that, the room of scientists and engineers erupted into a frenzy of cheering, hollering and clapping. Goosebumps instantly popped up all over Sophie's arms and neck. It overwhelmed the children. They knew what they did was special, but they had not expected this reaction. The applause went on for several minutes. It felt much longer.

Finally, when the cheering died down, Dr Millson spoke. "Sophie, Jack, Sahil, Leena, Biggles and Codey, we have been analysing the initial data from your mission. Do you have any idea what you have achieved? The mission was supposed to be a routine trip to investigate how children cope with space travel. You have made first contact with an intelligent alien civilisation! You have answered the age-old question of whether we are alone in the Universe!"

For the first time, Sophie was speechless. Jack decided to respond. "All part of the job, Dr Millson." He saluted the crowd, who laughed and applauded again.

"After all of your efforts, we want you to relax," Dr Millson continued. "We are sending a ship to you to bring you home. They should be with you in a couple of hours. Try to get some rest until they arrive."

Sophie finally managed to speak. "Thank you, Dr Millson. Thank you, everyone, for giving us this chance."

"We will see you soon. There are a lot of people that want to congratulate you."

The call ended. The kids got lost in their thoughts for a moment before Leena broke the silence. "So, what now?"

"This could be our last couple of hours alone," said Sahil, "I think we should have one last game of Football World Cup!"

"Yes!" shouted Leena.

The kids gathered in the virtual playroom. Sahil had linked Codey into the game's interfaces and created a programme to let him practice at 1000 times normal speed.

Jack, meanwhile, found the headset he adapted for Biggles. Before landing on Hope, he invented a game called 'Walk in a Park', which was supposed to be as relaxing as it sounds, only Biggles spent most of the time chasing virtual geese.

They started the match. Biggles sprinted around and occasionally nosed the ball. The children were passing the ball between them with ease, with plenty of clear communication. In the first match, they won 7-0, and after several victories, they made it into the final. "If this is our last game, we need to increase the difficulty level," said Sophie. "Let's have a real challenge!"

Sahil adjusted the settings, and the computer-controlled players were now much faster. Leena started dribbling with the ball but was wiped out by a sliding tackle.

Leena's face turned bright red, and she charged at the computer player, sliding at him from behind. She hooked one foot around the ball and won it back cleanly. She passed it forwards to Sahil, who took a first-time shot which the goalkeeper saved, and the ball went behind for a corner. Jack came running up from defence to join the crowd of players in the penalty area. Sahil took the corner, and Jack jumped high above the other players as if he were on Hope and headed the ball into the corner of the goal.

However, the computer passing was much better now, and within the next few minutes, they had scored two quick goals.

"Come on!" cried Jack. "We can't let our last game be a defeat."

In the second half, the six of them battled for every ball. Even Biggles seemed to be getting the idea of what he had to do. The children had to defend for most of the half. With a few minutes to go, Leena spotted a chance and intercepted a pass. She kicked it through to Sophie, who was running clear of the defenders. Codey surprised everyone by sprinting from the back to join Sophie. Sophie pretended she would shoot to fool the goalkeeper and then played a pass to Codey, who kicked it into the open goal.

"Yeessssss!" yelled Jack.

"Come on, let's go for the winner!" shouted Sophie.

The other team kicked off, and Sahil charged at them and won the ball by intercepting a pass. He played it to Jack on the wing, who was now bored of defending and wanted to score himself. Jack tried running at the defenders, but there were too many, so he turned and played it to Codey, who passed it straight to Sophie in the middle. Sophie played a perfect pass between two defenders to Leena, who was running into the penalty area. She hit the shot hard, but it hit the goalkeeper on the leg and bounced across the face of the goal. Out of nowhere, Biggles came sprinting into the box and launched himself into the ball, nosing it straight into the empty goal.

"Biggles scores the winner!" shouted Sahil. "I don't believe it!"

They all rushed over to hug Biggles. Jack lifted him over his head in celebration. Back in the real world, the children's communicators were beeping. The ship from Space Command had arrived.

"Flourish, this is Alpha 7. Are you receiving?"

Sophie responded, still out of breath from the goal celebrations. "Er, hi Alpha 7, this is Flourish. We will be with you in five minutes."

Chapter Twenty-One
Alpha 7

Leena rushed back to the control deck, followed closely by the others, and tapped the beeping button on her monitor. "Sophie, Alpha 7 are requesting permission to dock in cargo bay 2."

"I suppose we should let them," replied Sophie. "Open the cargo bay doors, and we can all go down and welcome them."

The children waited outside the cargo bay. The familiar scent of rocket fuel filled the corridor. They heard blasts of the Alpha 7 rockets as the ship manoeuvred into the bay, and a loud clang reverberated through Flourish when it touched down inside.

"It's going to be strange to see other humans again!" said Jack, as they waited for the bay to repressurise.

The red light above the door turned green to confirm the cargo bay external doors were closed and the air pressure and oxygen levels were suitable. Sophie entered to find the Alpha 7 spaceship parked inside. It was not much larger than Spacebug but nowhere near as modern looking. Several minor dents were evident in the dull-grey bodywork, and the Space Command logo was faded to the point where it was barely visible.

The Captain, a thin man with a receding ginger hairline, emerged from the main door and introduced himself in a Scottish accent. "Well, hello, my young colleagues. My name is Commander Peter Turner. Do you have any idea how excited everyone is about what you've discovered?"

"Hello, Commander Turner. Sophie Williams. I'm getting the feeling it's going to be a bit crazy on Earth?"

"Please, Sophie, call me Pete. Aye, crazy is an understatement. Do you know how many planets I've visited where there has been absolutely nothing of real interest? Most of the planets I go to, we can't even land on them." Pete started shaking his head whilst looking along the line of children. "And you bloody kids go and discover intelligent life in your first trip!"

Pete's crewmates emerged from the ship and introduced themselves. The pilot was a Chinese lady called Yan Li. Sophie couldn't help noticing how pretty she was. Her delicate facial features and jet-black hair tied back in a ponytail made her look young, although Sophie guessed she must be at least in her late twenties to be a fully-trained Space Command pilot. Jack and Sahil seemed in awe of her and smiled at each other when Yan Li emerged from the ship. Leena's eyes narrowed.

Yan Li spoke in a soft Chinese accent. "It's an honour to meet all of you. Leena, I can't wait to hear more about your meteor landing. It sounds like an amazing achievement. Congratulations."

Leena's scowl softened with Yan Li's complement.

Next, a scary-looking man with big muscles and a shaved head emerged. He introduced himself in a Russian accent as Dimitri Oleg, the ship's engineer. As Sophie shook his hand, she felt his skin was hard and leathery. Jack stuck his chest out, and his voice seemed to drop several octaves as he introduced himself. It looked like a competition as to who could grip the hardest during the handshake.

The last person to emerge was a lady with dark skin, braided black hair and a huge smile. "Hi everyone, I'm

Nalla Magoro. I'm in charge of wellbeing at Space Command. I'd like to speak to you all individually as soon as possible, starting with you first, Sophie, if that's okay?"

Pete, Dimitri and Yan Li went up to the control deck to set the ship on course for Earth. The others went to the dining area for lunch. Sophie invited Nalla to her room so they could talk privately.

"Please, have a seat," said Sophie, swinging the chair around from the desk and pointing it at the bed, which she then perched on.

"Thank you, Sophie. So, you've been through quite an experience! How are you feeling?"

Sophie shook her head and let out a small laugh. "Honestly? I have no idea. Proud. Excited. Overwhelmed. Grateful to have done this."

Nalla leant forwards. "What else, Sophie?" It was clear that she wanted to dig below the surface, and Sophie felt ready to let her.

"Relieved and, er, confused."

"What are you relieved about?"

"That we survived! And that we're coming home. I thought we might...." Sophie paused, closed her eyes for a moment and swallowed, before regaining her composure and continuing, "never see our families again. And relieved that we managed to save all the Hopian creatures."

"Of course. And what are you confused about?"

Sophie hesitated. She knew this would all be written up and shared with Space Command, and she still didn't want to sound crazy, but she couldn't keep it to herself any longer.

"The leader of the alien people, the Hopians as we call them, I'm convinced she communicated with me before we left Earth."

"How?"

"You're not going to believe this, but in my dreams."

Sophie told Nalla about the visions that she dreamt back in her little bedroom in Wales. Frustratingly, Nalla provided no clue as to what she thought about the dreams. All she did was take notes. However, it still felt good to tell someone.

Nalla looked at the picture on Sophie's desk. "This is your father?"

"Yes. He passed away over two years ago."

"I know. I'm sorry. I bet you miss him a lot?"

"He is still with me. I talk to him in my mind quite often. Talking about it with Sahil, Leena and Jack has also helped a lot." Sophie then remembered Leena recognising the Space Command background in her dad's picture. "Did you know him?"

Nalla responded quickly, almost instinctively. "Yes, I knew Mike. He was a great man."

"So, did he work at Space Command?"

"Er, I'm not sure if he was an employee, but I did meet him there," replied Nalla, who started to avoid eye contact with Sophie.

"When? And how many times?"

"I don't think I'm the best person to discuss this with, Sophie. I'll try to arrange for you to have a follow-up conversation with colleagues."

"But this is what I find so annoying!" snapped Sophie. "You are supposed to be here for my wellbeing! I can deal with the aliens, the near-death experiences and even my crazy dreams. The thing that keeps me awake at night is wondering what my dad was doing at Space Command, what his top-secret work involved and how he died! My mum won't tell me anything, and neither will any of you!" Tears streamed down Sophie's cheeks.

Nalla scribbled down more notes and handed Sophie a tissue. "I'm sorry, Sophie. I understand your frustration. Please, leave it with me."

Sophie took a few moments to recover from her outburst before returning to the dining area. "Sahil, she wants to speak to you next. You can use my room."

Sahil finished the last of his pasta, washed it down with orange juice and headed along the corridor towards Sophie's room.

"You look upset, Sophie," said Leena. "Are you ok?"

Sophie grabbed a plate of pasta and sat down. "I'm fine."

"I can see you're not. You said it's good to talk about emotions, so why won't you tell me about yours?"

Sophie let out a deep sigh. "You're right, Leena. I'll tell you, but please keep it to yourselves." Leena and Jack leant forwards. "It was about my dad. I just get the feeling no one wants to tell me what he did or how he died."

"Maybe they don't know," suggested Jack.

Sophie shook her head as she added pepper to her pasta. "He was working for Space Command. Someone must know something. It's very odd."

The kids relaxed for the rest of the afternoon. Sophie pulled a bean bag over to one of the viewing windows and watched Earth approaching. Due to the spin of Flourish, the tiny blue world was moving around in small circles. It was strange seeing the whole planet, looking no bigger than Sophie's thumb. It appeared so peaceful from such a distance. Pete's words echoed around Sophie's head. 'Crazy is an understatement.' *Maybe I should just relax as much as I can before the mayhem starts.*

The peace was shattered by Codey thundering past on the wheels built into his knees with Biggles running along behind, looking tired.

"Codey, do you have to do that now?" shouted Sophie.

"Biggles needs his daily exercise quota. So far, he has reached 38%, but if you prefer I can continue later?"

"Please!"

Codey released Biggles from the leash and disappeared off down the corridor. Sophie called Biggles over for a cuddle. He seemed extremely grateful.

Watching Earth growing in the viewing window, sat on the beanbag and stroking Biggles, Sophie tried to comprehend what had happened to her, not just in the last few days but over the past year. She had come a long way since starting secondary school in September, when she didn't talk much to anyone and her classmates barely noticed her. Through applying for the mission, Sophie became one of the most well-known and popular children in the school, which was hard enough to comprehend. Now she was going to be one of the most famous children on the planet. *What will life be like on Earth now? What will I do next?* It was an exciting thought rather than a scary one. *Think of the possibilities!*

She decided to avoid overthinking it. *Just take it in small steps.* The circular movement of Earth in the distance started to feel hypnotic. Her eyes were heavy, and she let them close.

She found herself underwater once more. The blurry image of the Hopian came into view through the bright light.

"Sophie."

"Hello again. Are your people okay?"

"Yes, thanks to you, Sophie. You saved us. Thank you."

"What's your name?"

"I can no longer contact you, Sophie. It's not safe. I just wanted to say thank you and goodbye."

"Wait! Why is it not safe? Please, just tell me your name."

"Call me...Trista. Goodbye, Sophie."

"Wait, please..."

Sophie woke. There were so many more questions she wanted to ask. *How was Trista talking to me in my dreams? Why wouldn't it be safe for Trista to contact me again?* At least this time, there were no burning rocks and no fiery destruction. Everything was good. Biggles turned his head to Sophie and licked her cheek before nuzzling down for another nap.

Sophie's eyes closed again, and this time her dreams felt different – as if they were her own. She was at school, helping Josh with his next application to Space Command. Then she was in the headteacher's office, and Mrs Jenkins kept telling her how wonderful her adventure had been for the 'reputation of the school'. She dreamt of her mum, who was delighted to have her back at home and wouldn't release her from a warm hug. She dreamt of her dad, who was walking towards his garden workshop. He turned to look at Sophie and then spoke in his clear, deep voice. "I'm so proud of you, sweetheart."

"Ladies and gentlemen, boys and girls, dogs and robots." Sophie woke again, this time due to Commander Turner's thick Glaswegian accent being broadcast on all the ship's communicators. "We will soon be arriving at a small, rather boring planet called Earth. Please make your way to the control deck."

"Come on, Biggles, let's get ready for the mayhem of Earth!" said Sophie, wrestling her way out of the beanbag.

Chapter Twenty-Two
Home

Climbing the ladder and seeing Pete, Yan Li and Dimitri sat at the control deck felt strange to Sophie. Pete was sat in *her* chair. There were additional fold-down seats at the back of the cabin. After strapping Biggles into his chair, Sophie pulled one down and buckled in.

Leena was next to emerge from the top of the ladder. She had a similar reaction to Sophie, looking awkwardly at Yan Li sat in her pilot's seat. By force of habit, Leena floated towards the pilot chair and then had to push herself towards the rear of the cabin. "Sorry," she muttered.

Jack was less subtle when he floated into the control deck. "Hey, Dimitri, what are you doing in my seat, dude?"

Dimitri ignored him and continued to check his instruments.

"Come on, big guy!" Jack persisted. "Don't make me fight you for it."

Dimitri glanced at Jack with the slightest hint of a grin.

Pete answered on his behalf. "Sorry, Jack, we are under strict instructions to take control of the landing. Orders from above and all that."

"Are you saying after landing Flourish on a tiny spinning meteor, you don't trust me to land back at the Spaceport?" said Leena.

Sophie smiled. She could tell Leena was joking, but it would have sounded serious to those unfamiliar with her accent.

Sahil and Nalla arrived on the control deck. Sahil instinctively sat in his chair, leaving Nalla with one of the few remaining fold-down seats at the back.

"Sahil, I think you're supposed to sit here with us and let Nalla have your chair," said Sophie.

"Oh, my apologies Nalla, please be my guest and take this seat."

Nalla smiled. "It's fine, Sahil. You will make better use of all the controls than I would!"

"Oh man!" exclaimed Jack. "Sahil gets his chair back, whilst the rest of us just get the cheap seats!"

"Jack, be quiet!" said Sophie and Pete at the same moment.

Coming into land on Earth was more spectacular than the launch. Even though they were rotated at an unfamiliar angle and half covered in cloud, Sophie recognised the British Isles coming into view on the main screen. Slowly, her home country of Wales grew as Pete opened a channel to Space Command engineers. The deceleration tugged Sophie's internal organs as Yan Li fired the rockets to slow the ship and expertly guide it towards Pad 9, as instructed by Space Command engineers on the ground. The moment of touchdown was barely noticeable.

"That was a nice landing Yan Li," remarked Leena.

Yan Li smiled. "Thanks, Leena. I have been doing this for a while!"

Pete turned to the children and outlined the next steps. "They need to scan us for any alien bugs that could wipe out humanity, so you won't be able to hug your family and friends immediately, but it doesn't take long. They will also sterilise the ship and all your belongings. Then I imagine, because you are the first humans to make contact with aliens, and the fact that you happen to be children, there might be just a little bit of media interest!"

Jack grinned. Sophie could tell he was probably rehearsing one of his funny speeches in his mind.

"Pete, please can I have a minute alone with my crew before it all starts?" asked Sophie.

"Aye, this will probably be your last chance. Make the most of it."

The four adults left the kids, Codey and Biggles on the control deck. Feeling the full effects of gravity on this part of the ship felt strange to Sophie, and it took a huge effort to haul herself up from her seat. She turned to the others.

"I don't know about you three, but I have mixed feelings about leaving the ship. It's going to be weird back on Earth." Sophie said.

"Do you think we will go to space together again soon?" asked Leena.

"Who knows. Maybe we will have the chance to do another mission together one day. But what I do know is I have made three of the best friends I will ever have. Whatever happens, we are going to keep in touch. I want to play more Football World Cup!"

The children, Biggles and Codey left the ship and went through the bio scanners, which showed they were free of dangerous bacteria. Dr Millson was waiting for them on the other side with a beaming ear-to-ear smile and embraced the children all at once. "The more data we analyse from your mission, the more amazed we all are," she said breathlessly.

Sophie gasped when she noticed an elderly gentleman behind Dr Millson, who she recognised immediately as Professor Yang, Director of Space Command.

"My colleagues," announced Professor Yang, in his slow, authoritative, Chinese accent. "Welcome home. Congratulations. We have a special meeting planned for you. First, please may I have a quick discussion with your captain in private?"

Professor Yang led Sophie into a side room, closed the door and invited her to sit.

"It's an honour to meet you, Professor," said Sophie, bowing slightly before taking a seat.

He paced up and down the room as he spoke. "No, Sophie, the honour is mine. You have now achieved more than I or anyone at Space Command ever have, and possibly ever will. You will get a lot of attention. Will you be ok with this?"

The enormity of Sophie's achievements was starting to sink in, along with the realisation of how different her life would be compared to when she left Earth. Her stomach was turning over. She reverted to what she thought would be her most professional answer. "Yes, of course. I wanted to inspire other children to believe in themselves, so now I can't wait to tell my story."

"I knew we chose the right captain. I'm also aware that we owe you some answers. We are considering the possibility that you were contacted by the extra-terrestrial beings, as you reported to Nalla in the debriefing session. We are currently investigating this fascinating development."

"You believe me, Professor? I was worried you might think I was crazy!" said Sophie as she felt her cheeks reddening.

"Of course, I believe you, Sophie, and you most certainly are not crazy. Something not understood is not necessarily impossible. It may relate to the work of your father."

Sophie's smile dropped. "What do you mean?"

Professor Yang pulled a chair over and sat facing Sophie, very close to her. He hesitated before speaking, thinking through every word. "This information is highly sensitive, and I would be grateful if you could keep it to yourself. But you, more than anyone, have a right to know, and I apologise for not informing you of this previously. Your father was working on the possibility of transmitting messages between star systems. Michael had some interesting theories."

"Are you saying it could be because of my father's work that the Hopians were able to speak to me in my dreams?"

"We are investigating this possibility."

Sophie decided to ask the question she had been wondering for more than two years. "How did he die,

Professor?"

Professor Yang hesitated. His eyes looked full of sorrow. "Your father's death is still being investigated." He let out a short but noticeable sigh. "The truth is, we are still not sure. Please be patient in your search for answers, Sophie. I promise you this, you and your mother will be the first to know when we have something meaningful to tell you."

Sophie's eyes were beginning to glaze. "Thank you."

Professor Yang took Sophie's hand. "Your father was a great man, Sophie, but his work was highly confidential. As I say, please do not discuss it further. All will be explained to you just as soon as we can."

"I understand," replied Sophie whilst maintaining direct eye contact, despite the tears forming.

"Are you ready to face the public? There is a lot of people who would like to hear from you!"

Sophie swallowed and wiped her eyes on her sleeve. "Yes, I am."

The other three children were chatting with Dr Millson when Sophie and Professor Yang joined them. Sahil was babbling excitedly about some of the experiences, including riding on the back of the dinobirds. Dr Millson led them along the corridors and to a door. She paused before entering.

"We have assembled a bit of a crowd, but please don't be intimidated. I will direct you to your chairs on the stage. Codey, when we enter, please stand to the left of the table on the stage."

"Yes, Dr Millson," replied Codey. Sophie thought his voice actually sounded a little nervous, or maybe it was just her imagination.

"I will hold Biggles, and all that will happen is Professor Yang would like to say a few words. Is that ok with everyone?"

"Yes, ma'am!" said Jack.

"Fine with me, thank you," replied Sahil.

Leena just nodded. Sophie caught sight of her reflection in an office window and adjusted her hair slightly. "Yes, let's go!"

Dr Millson led the group into a vast conference centre. There were hundreds of people. As they made their way along the stage, flashes of camera lights dazzled them, and a roar from the crowd seemed to lift the roof from the building. Sophie sat in her chair and held her hands under the desk to hide that they were shaking. The applause continued for many minutes. The kids looked at each other in disbelief. Jack was smiling from ear to ear, Sahil was laughing, and Leena was waving to someone she knew in the crowd. Looking closer, Sophie realised it must have been Leena's parents. She then scanned the audience, searching for any familiar faces. *Where is she? Where's mum?*

Before she had time to spot anyone she knew, Professor Yang was handed a microphone and started speaking in his slow, deep, deliberate voice. "Ladies and gentlemen. What we have observed has taken space exploration beyond our wildest dreams. The question of whether we are alone in the Universe has been answered. Thanks to these six individuals, we now know about Planet Hope and the intelligent and fascinating beings that live there. These beings are capable of sophisticated communication and have built spectacular cities. They could detect a large meteor on a collision course with their planet, but they had no defence against it. However, it just so happened that these four children, this dog and this robot were visiting, and whilst there saved them from certain annihilation."

The crowd erupted in applause and cheering once again. When it eventually died down, Professor Yang turned to Sahil. "I would like Sahil to stand up, please."

Sahil was surprised to hear his name. His eyes widened as he stood. "Sahil, you have gathered so much scientific data from the mission that scientists around the world will be busy for years. First, you recorded huge quantities of information from the gas planet and the K2-18 star. You collected samples from Hope, the planet that you so appropriately named. You came up with a brilliant way of communicating with the Hopian people. It was you, Sahil, that detected the meteor heading for the planet. You then gathered data about the meteor and helped code a true simulation of it and the ship. Sahil, I am privileged to present you with this medal, the highest possible scientific award that Space Command can issue."

The crowd cheered and applauded. Sahil attempted a slightly awkward bow as Professor Yang put a medal over his head. He waved at the crowd. A small section was cheering wildly, which Sophie suspected was his family.

"Next, Jack. Please stand."

Jack took to his feet. It seemed physically impossible for his smile to grow any wider, but he managed it.

"Jack, I have been speaking to many of our most senior engineers at Space Command. They all agree that what you did to reconfigure the rockets to enable you to catch the gas planet was nothing short of astonishing. Not many of them would have thought of it, let alone could do it. You then realised that you could produce more rocket fuel on the surface of Hope, and you came up with the plan to change the path of the meteor. Jack, it gives me huge pleasure to present you with our highest award for engineering."

Jack performed his now famous salute. Sophie recognised his brother in the crowd. He was punching the air and cheering.

"I don't want to forget our two non-human members of the team. Biggles and Codey, please step forwards."

Codey stepped forwards. Biggles stayed exactly where he was until Dr Millson gave him a little push.

"Codey, we programmed you to look after the children and the ship and to help with repairs. You have gone way beyond your programming. It is encouraging that robots can learn how to help so much with these types of missions. I also understand that you are getting rather good at hide and seek now?"

The crowd laughed. Codey responded. "Yes, I like hide and seek. I also like my team. I think I will miss them now it has finished."

"Don't worry, Codey. We have many exciting plans for you. We have never before awarded a medal to a robot, but I'm awarding you a special medal in light of your brilliant work on this mission."

Professor Yang turned to Biggles. "Biggles, you were always a very popular dog here at Space Command, and we knew you were the right companion to help keep the children calm on the long trip. What we didn't realise is that you would be crucial to the survival of your team. If I understand correctly, you sniffed out the materials needed to make fuel on Hope and somehow communicated this to the alien beings?

We thought about giving you a medal, but we decided you would more appreciate this special treat."

Professor Yang leant down and gave Biggles his favourite treat, choco-meat biscuits, and a pat on the head. Biggles decided not to wait for the end of the ceremony. He crunched away.

"Now, Leena, please stand."

Leena took a deep breath and rose to her feet.

"Leena, we knew before the mission started that you were an exceptional pilot. However, little did we realise the demands that would be placed on you during this mission. Firstly, you had to fly incredibly close to the surface of a vast gas planet to maximise your speed, a manoeuvre that few pilots have ever attempted. You executed it perfectly. Then on approach to Hope, you collided with the large bird creature, the dinobird as you call them. No one could have predicted that they would be there. Despite flying a broken ship with no power, you managed to control the landing and save the lives of your team."

Leena looked uncomfortable with all the attention. Sophie smiled, realising what was coming next.

"What you were then required to do, Leena, no pilot on Earth would have wanted to do. You had to perform a near impossible manoeuvre, and the price for failure would have been the almost certain loss of a planet of intelligent life, as well as your own life and the lives of your team. You came up with an ingenious way of turning something virtually impossible into something possible. And then you did it. You landed a large starship on a small meteor with precision accuracy. In doing so, you have drastically changed the course of history. I am presenting you with the highest award a pilot can achieve, and can I say it feels like nowhere near enough."

Leena looked out to her parents. Tears were streaming down their faces. She couldn't contain her emotions and unexpectedly blurted out a response. "It was only thanks to my team that I could have done that. I love them all so much. It was Sophie, particularly, that helped me to believe in myself."

"Quite right, Leena, thank you," said Professor Yang with a smile. "Sophie, as you may have guessed, it's now your turn to stand."

It now felt more like dinobirds rather than butterflies fluttering inside Sophie's tummy. Whilst standing, she noticed her Headteacher, Mrs Jenkins, and then her English teacher, Mr Galway, in the audience. Looking along the line, she realised her whole class were there, including Josh, Dylan and Adian, who were clapping hysterically and wolf-whistling. She gasped as she then spotted her mum, whose makeup was a mess because she was crying so much.

"Sophie, you held your team together and got the very best out of each of them. Your decision making was perfect. I know Dr Millson instructed you not to take unnecessary risks, but you recognised that sometimes risks must be taken for the greater good. Your handling of the first communications with the Hopian people has ensured that we have not only discovered an alien species, but we have secured a friendship with them. Sophie, we are awarding you with the highest award for leadership that we can issue."

Sophie leant forward to accept the medal whilst considering what to say. "Thank you, Professor Yang. Thank you to everyone at Space Command."

"Sophie, it's us that should be thanking all of you. Thank you for giving humankind these discoveries. Thank you for inspiring children and adults from all corners of the Earth. Thank you for giving us Hope!"

Afterword

Thank you for reading this book. I hope you enjoyed it. If you did, then all the effort has been worthwhile.

Please let me know what you thought by leaving a review on Amazon and Goodreads. And, of course, tell your friends about it! You can send them this link:

http://mybook.to/SpaceKids

Space Kids 2 is on the way. If you would like the first two chapters right now, subscribe at alannettleton.com and I'll send them to you by email.

Thank you.

Printed in Great Britain
by Amazon

77829688R00154